## Sleeping pretty

A murder victim wreathed in white and found in the middle of a lonely Highland loch. A suicide victim hanging from the end of a rope on the shore.

The crime is solved before David Fyfe reaches the scene, except the solution is wrong and the tale is infinitely more tangled and sinister than it seems at first sight.

There are more than enough false leads and stray facts in the investigation to occupy Fyfe's full attention. But his mind isn't really on the job because he is on the case with Detective Inspector Moya McBain, a late developer troubled by unrequited ambition and a wayward sex drive.

A crime of passion killed the two people by the loch. More illicit passion is generated between Fyfe and McBain as they dutifully try to resist the mutual attraction. But it's not easy and as the extraordinary truth emerges from behind a smokescreen of corrupt respectability they find themselves caught up in an uncompromising flow of events, moving rapidly towards an ultimately unexpected and brutal consummation.

# SLEEPING PRETTY

## William Paul

Constable · London

First published in Great Britain 1995
by Constable & Company Ltd
3 The Lanchesters, 162 Fulham Palace Road
London W6 9ER
Copyright © 1995 by William Paul
The right of William Paul to be
identified as the author of this work
has been asserted by him in accordance
with the Copyright, Designs and Patents Act 1988
ISBN 0 09 474050 X
Set in Linotron Palatino 10 pt by
CentraCet Ltd, Cambridge
Printed in Great Britain by
Hartnolls Ltd, Bodmin

A CIP catalogue record for this book is
available from the British Library

# 1

He ducked below the low lintel of the cottage door. It was dark inside. A blast of loud unintelligible music surrounded him and made him hold his hands up to his face as an instinctive form of defence. He hesitated, blinking behind the thick glasses he wore, allowing his eyes to adjust to the gloom. He rolled his shoulders to fight off cramp and opened his mouth to be able to breathe more easily. He moved along the corridor.

The air in the cottage was almost opaque. It had a curious taste as he sucked it down his throat into his lungs. He felt for the light switch and flicked it up and down several times, but it didn't work.

The loudness of the music was making the floorboards vibrate. A sliver of doubt about what he was doing inserted itself like a sharp blade into his mind. For an instant the air congealed into solidity and he choked on it, coughing harshly. Then he recovered and was at the living-room door. It was already open. The music fled out of the room, streaming round him like an invisible wind.

Directly opposite he could see the dull orange glow of a damped-down fire. To one side the flickering green and red display lights of the CD player danced like thin electronic flames. On the other side was an armchair and sitting in it Laura, his fantasy lover.

She was dressed all in white. Her head was bowed. Her face was hidden by dark tumbling hair. She seemed not to notice him. This was the Laura he had watched develop from a child into a precocious teenager and then a beautiful, irresistibly sexy young woman. Somewhere along the line the loyalty of the family friend had got hopelessly mixed up with

5

the gut-aching lust of the unrequited lover. He had been frightened to do anything about it, too frightened of his own emotions and the consequences it might have for his own neatly-ordered life. Ron Gilchrist was too old for her, too middle-class, too respectable, too married, too frightened to change. But then she had come looking for him, and he could not resist her. He did not want to and he did not try to. So when she had called for help earlier that day he could only respond instantly.

The long, frantic drive north in his Range Rover had ended outside the whitewashed cottage in a short skid on the loose gravel of the approach road beside the familiar car already parked there. At the southern tip of Loch Maree the rounded mass of Slioch, 3000-foot high, had reared from the rocky landscape to guide him.

Gilchrist drove fast, foot pressed to the boards, knuckles pale, passing everything else on the road. A hotel flashed by. Its windows glowed like the cutaway holes in the lampshade they had by the fire at home, the one with the Victorian inn and the stagecoach pulled by straining, wide-eyed horses. Then into the forest, entering a black avenue with trees on each side like the ribs of some great monster's belly, and at the end of it the white walls of the newly familiar cottage glowed in the headlights. A front tyre bumped clumsily over the brick-lined verge of the flower-beds, flattening a row of beautiful blue irises. Swirling dust rose around the wheel arches of the Range Rover, hugging its metallic contours.

Already from the driving seat he could hear the loud music inside. It was muffled by the white stone walls and curtained windows. Twenty yards away on his right the loch shone blackly under a clear but rapidly darkening sky. A rowing-boat was pulled up on the narrow shingle beach. Oars projected from its sides like folded wings. In the middle of the loch he could just make out the humps of the wooded islands like whales lying at rest in the water. Beyond them was the dead-end vertical wall of the far shore.

And all the time he was remembering the keening edge of desperation in the voice over the phone four hours before.

'She's acting strangely, Ron,' she kept repeating. 'She really is. I don't know what she might do next. I've never seen her like this before. I'm scared, Ron. I'm so scared.'

And here Laura was, sitting alone in the roaring half-darkness. Around her the black iron fender and the undersides of the exposed ceiling beams shone darkly. Selina the black cat, a smudge in the darkness, sat at her feet, watching him with glittering green eyes.

'Laura,' he said, entering the room. 'What's happened?'

The music drowned everything. His footsteps made no sound. The cat moved away silently. Gilchrist went forward. Her head seemed to move or maybe it was just his shadow passing over her. He reached for Laura's hand as he crouched down in front of her. His legs were sore and stiff from the hours of driving. Pains beset every muscle. He had to move slowly.

How often had he dreamed of being alone with Laura in a situation like this? How often had he secretly dreamed of lying beside her with her hair soft and warm on his chest and her fingers intertwined with his? When they ate together in restaurants he hoped people would think they were lovers. Every time they met he had hoped she would suddenly confess her secret desire for him. He was shocked when she did, rendered completely speechless, afraid that she was teasing him. But she was genuine and the affair had begun barely a month before.

It wasn't right. It wasn't decent. It would never last. But Gilchrist's conviction that if he waited patiently she would eventually turn to him had been proved right. No coercion had been necessary. It had been her decision alone, and it was not based on pity or sympathy. Now she had called him to rescue her in her hour of desperate need. He was proud to answer the call.

He would do as she wanted, he had decided, whatever it was. If she had committed murder he would help her cover it up. If she wanted him to kill on her behalf he would do so willingly. He had this idea in his mind that he was ashamed of because of its calculated cynicism, but if he helped Laura now he would have a firm hold over her. He would have the ability to control her, to demand sex on his own terms, to have her in his debt to do his bidding. It would be like having her on a leash.

7

The music seemed to slow and quieten. His ears were adjusting to the volume as his eyes had done to the light. The words suddenly started to make sense. *Lay lady lay*, sang Bob Dylan. *Lay across my big brass bed*.

Gilchrist took Laura's hand. It was cold and unresponsive. He brushed her hair away from her face and touched something hard that was sticking to it. Still she kept her head bowed. He put his fingers under her chin and gently tilted it upwards.

'What's the matter Laura,' he whispered. 'You can tell me.'

Her face came level with his. The whites of her eyes stared blankly into his. Reflections of the CD's electronic lights squirmed inside them. He saw the streak of dried blood running like a scar down the side of her face and the necklace of ugly purple bruises round her throat.

Fear of death seized his heart and squeezed unmercifully. The music swelled around him. The sound waves penetrated his body and entered his blood. He began to shake uncontrollably.

# 2

*Wednesday, 21.11*

Two guests tonight. Two ladies. Mrs Sutherland was one. An elderly grey-haired granny who had worn well and unexpectedly dropped dead at the age of ninety. Heart attack. Out like a light. 'Best way to go,' said her niece, an elderly woman herself with a pinched face and constant hacking cough that suggested her lights, too, might soon go out. Mrs Sutherland's corpse was safely screwed down in her oak coffin in rest room number one. She had been old. Her funeral would be a social occasion. A stray tear here and there, maybe, but no great display of grief. It was time for her to go.

The other guest was Miss Arnott. In rest room two, lying in the open silk-lined walnut coffin with her eyes closed and her hands folded neatly over her stomach. She had been an attractive young woman, mid-twenties, car crash victim in a nasty accident in the south of England, massive internal injuries, a week in coma as the life gradually leaked out of her. It had been a major job for the morticians to repair the facial damage and make Miss Arnott presentable for the procession of weeping friends and relatives. Her funeral would be a chaotic maelstrom of tortured emotions. She was too young. It was not her time to go.

Douglas Lambert was restless. He had come downstairs from the flat where he lived alone above the funeral parlour to do his unnecessary nightwatchman's rounds. There was, after all, nothing to steal and no possibility of escape for unsatisfied clients.

He looked in briefly on Mrs Sutherland's coffin in rest room one. He switched out the light and locked the door again behind him. He opened the door of rest room two. The scent of cut flowers took the edge off the chemical smell of air freshener. Miss Arnott was resting in peace under the chest-high concealed lighting on the wall. The expression on her face was somewhere between indifference and rapture. She was wearing a favourite dress, creamy ivory with a high neck and light blue piping on the sleeves. Her dark hair framed the chalk-white face which had just enough colour painted into it to make it seem half-alive. Diamond ear-rings sparkled. The lips were the palest of pinks. The merest touch of blusher on the cheeks, a hint of shadow on the closed eyelids. An overall puffiness of the skin was hardly noticeable. No scars were visible without inappropriately close scrutiny. She would not have looked out of place walking down a street among real live people.

Lambert looked down on Miss Arnott and meditated, as he always did, on the nature of death. In almost a lifetime in the family business dealing with dead bodies, young and old, he had never shaken off the little shiver of impending mortality that came with each solemn new encounter. He was a past master at sympathizing with those left behind. Had he not suffered the same when his wife died? And his son? He knew when to speak and when to remain silent. With Miss Arnott's bewildered parents all it had required was a quick explanation of the arrangements and a step back into obscurity. Others

9

might have, but they did not want to be comforted by a stranger. They did not want words of pity or of support. All they wanted was to be left alone with their daughter.

Lambert understood perfectly. He had seen every kind of reaction to untimely death, from meek acceptance to raging fury. It was never certain, never predictable, but experience had taught him it was always manageable. The funerals were prepared for the next day, limousines ready, intimations made. Mrs Sutherland went to the crematorium, Miss Arnott to St Andrew's church and Trinity cemetery. Final farewells. Lambert didn't do actual funerals any more. He left them to his staff, preferring to stay indoors in the background.

He took a small plastic battery-operated fan from his pocket and flicked it on. The blades whirred into invisibility with hardly a sound. He placed it on the dead woman's chest, pointing at her chin. Her hair shifted slightly in the stream of air. Miss Arnott's parents would be back first thing in the morning to sit with their daughter. It would not be nice if a layer of dust had settled on her face overnight. The fan would keep it clear.

He walked backwards to the door of the rest room. Upstairs in his home he would treat himself to some hot chocolate before retiring to bed with a good thriller. There it was again, the faint flutter of selfish fear in the pit of his belly. One day Lambert himself would lie in a coffin with a painted face while those left behind shuffled slowly past to pay their respects. His wife had gone before him. His son too, a boy so young and clean-limbed and full of potential. Then a second wife. And what about his daughter, his only daughter. An incongruous smile broke out on his face at the sight of Miss Arnott in front of him. She was a good job, a fine example of the mortician's art.

Ignore the inconvenient fact that she was dead and any parent would be proud of how she looked. The dead body was, to Lambert's coldly professional eye, in the kind of condition that made his job worthwhile. She was sleeping pretty.

# 3

Gilchrist was suddenly jerked to his feet. He had hold of Laura's hand. She was dragged off the chair by his involuntary movement. The crack of her forehead as it struck the bare floorboards cleaved like a pistol shot through the total background of pervasive loud music.

He would have screamed but a noose was tight around his neck silencing him. It pulled him up and swung him in a circle until he fell over. His glasses flew off. He caught a glimpse of two shadows struggling on the walls as he went down, arms flailing. One was his. The other belonged to his attacker. A third shadow lurked behind. The dancing coloured lights from the CD player were unnaturally elongated across his field of vision, a fairground streamer as though he was on a whirling roundabout. He spun helplessly in the centre of the room.

His knees hit first, then a shoulder, and then his face smacked into the floor. It stayed like that, his nose pressed hard against the sanded boards. The grain of the wood had formed a remarkably beautiful pattern. There was a knot in one plank in the form of a perfect whirlpool.

Gilchrist clawed at his throat but could not get a grip on the unforgiving noose that had encircled it. His oxygen supply was being shut off. He tried to move his head off the floor but it was clamped there and held by a tremendous weight. Somebody was kneeling on his neck. He couldn't see them but he knew they were there. He could imagine the distorted face, the spittle-flecked lips, as the deadly noose was twisted tighter and tighter. There was absolutely nothing he could do to stop it. What would his wife think when she found out? She would discover that he and Laura were lovers. He wished he could be alive to see her face. What would she think of him then?

He could just make out one of Laura's feet behind him. It

wasn't her fault then. She hadn't betrayed him. She remained gentle, considerate and loving to the end. She was dead too, a victim just like him.

The foot was dainty and pink in the glow of the meagre firelight. The cat padded into sight and lay on its side on the floor at Laura's feet, its green eyes watching him disinterestedly. Selina licked each front paw in turn as Gilchrist's body jerked convulsively in its death spasms.

His vision dimmed. Dylan loudly demanded to know: *How d'ya feel?* His hearing failed. The music faded into the distance. His brain gave up the struggle of commanding oxygen-deprived limbs to fight back.

He thought of himself as a cat going to sleep in front of the fire, curled up and absorbed into Laura's lap. It wasn't painful. It wasn't difficult. He merged into the fondest of memories. He just closed his eyes and quietly died.


# 4


*Wednesday, 21.25*


The hourglass was a Victorian folly, an egg-timer on steroids. It was four-foot tall and its huge glass bulbs were contained inside a mahogany framework of barley sugar legs and cross-struts carved with all sorts of queer cherubs, bunches of grapes and dragons' heads. The sand contained in it was greyish brown and took ninety-six hours or four days to pass through the filament waist in an uninterrupted flow.

Eddie Illingworth had found it in a junk shop when he was a teenager. He had made the mistake of appearing enthusiastic about buying it and had had to pay over the odds. It had accompanied him in his wanderings ever since, somehow surviving the worst excesses when other items he accumulated were broken or lost. It now stood on the floor of his bedroom at Tollcross in Edinburgh, gloriously out of place among the other flat-pack furniture, standing in splendid isolation on the azure blue carpet with bubble-mouthed fish woven into it that had been another impulse buy on a Canary Islands holiday during his recklessly indulgent youth.

Illingworth was pleased with himself. Another month was safely behind him, another magazine successfully compiled and edited. The final proof copies had arrived that morning ahead of schedule and he had spent the day on the phone ironing out the last few minor production wrinkles. It had taken all day and most of the evening but he had stuck at it even though his staff had uncharacteristically abandoned him, pleading prior engagements.

He couldn't argue with his dear, spaced-out sister Norma or she would have flattened him. She took off before he had finished his first bacon roll. Neither could he argue with his advertising director Patricia. She was the boss's wife, after all, and she wanted the afternoon off. The boss himself took a bundle of proof copies and disappeared without saying a word. He stayed on alone and did it all himself.

Illingworth was in his late thirties but heart bypass surgery had aged him prematurely. He was a big, heavy man with unfashionably long hair and a still handsome but careworn face. He had held down good jobs in newspapers, but never for long. He had moved into public relations but that hadn't really worked for him. The magazine job came as a life-saver when he believed he was on the scrap heap after his operation.

He had never heard of the magazine, *Ethereal*. He knew nothing about reincarnation and even less about New Age philosophy but big sister Norma, who was the secretary in the office, kept him right. At least he had a healthy belief in the paranormal, was a professional bluffer and a good liar. He was given the editor's job because the owner, who seemed a bit divorced from reality, liked him. It wasn't a huge responsibility. There weren't any staff to order about. Except Norma who knew more about the operation than he ever would. And Pat, the boss's wife, who worked quietly away on her own and filled eighty per cent of the pages.

He had been doing it for two years and his lack of detailed knowledge on the subject had proved a help rather than a hindrance. He had presided over a subscription rise of fifty per cent. He didn't really know what he was doing right, but he kept doing it and taking the credit for it. What else were editors for?

In his bedroom he took hold of the heavy wooden frame of the hourglass and hoisted it off the floor. Whenever a magazine was completed he went through the same ceremony, allowing himself a four-day binge to flush out his nervous system. It had become a tradition. He didn't drink often but when he did, he did it with a vengeance. When the sand stopped running he would sober up. Until then he could be a different person.

The hourglass somersaulted in his hands and went back down on the floor into the same four indentations in the carpet. For a few minutes he stood watching the thin stream of sand trickling through into the empty glass bulb. Then he went to get himself a drink.

# 5

*Wednesday, 21.56*

The rope was tied to the corner post of the black cast-iron fender in front of the smouldering fire. Individual loose strands of hemp were picked out in the halo thrown by the weak firelight. The rope ran diagonally up to a central roof beam, over it and vertically down to Ron Gilchrist's neck. His body was standing on the seat of a chair in the middle of the room. It hung in a curve, bent at the knees and ankles like a parachutist frozen in the act of hitting the ground.

The CD lights flickered and flashed as the music played loudly. Dylan sang how it was just like a woman.

> *And she aches just like a woman,*
> *but she breaks just like a little girl.*

Laura's lifeless body had been lifted from the floor where she had fallen. Her head lolled backwards on the armchair. Her

14

sightless eyes were turned towards Gilchrist. Selina the cat was on the floor by the fire, watching too, its fur outlined in its own feline-shaped halo.

The shadows on the wall copied the motion of a leg kicking out. The chair tumbled away, the sound of it making no impression on the music. Gilchrist spun and swung. His limp arms jumped and flapped until slowly, very slowly, the momentum faded and the body drooped in mid-air, the toes of its shoes almost scraping the ground.

As the body stopped swinging the music track came to an end. A few seconds of silence was followed by the click of the random selector in operation. The rustle of an expectant crowd echoed out into the room. The twanging of a guitar and then the shrill notes of a harmonica. *How many roads must a man walk down*, Bob Dylan sang, and the applause was redoubled as the tune was recognized.

Gilchrist's hanging corpse gave a final twist to the left and back again. Then it was motionless. The black cat climbed into Laura's lap and settled down, laying its head on its paws and curling its tail round.

*The answer, my friends, is blowin' in the wind*, Dylan roared. *The answer is blowin' in the wind.*

# 6

*Wednesday, 22.30*

Another evening, another row. Ian Dalglish stood by the kitchen door putting on his coat. His bottom lip stuck out like a petulant child's. God, he could be so infuriating. If anything had been to hand Moya McBain would have flung it at him.

'I'm going then,' he said.

'Bloody well go,' she replied.

'I am. Thanks for a mediocre night out.'

'I'd like to say the same only it wasn't as good as that.'

'You can be a thrawn bitch at times Moya.'

15

'I try my best.'

The evening had begun promisingly enough with pizza at a restaurant in Inverness, then a quiet drink at a country hotel on the way back to Moya's house. It was a kiss-and-make-up occasion after their last argument. She had been expecting him to stay the night. The sheets were aired, the electric blanket was on, the sexy nightdress was ready. But somewhere along the line the niggling had started, backhanded insults had been traded, and the whole carefully constructed reconciliation collapsed around them. Dalglish was barely in the door at the house before he was on his way out again.

'I hope you and your career will be very happy together,' he said.

'At least the job is part of the twentieth century which is more than can be said for you.'

'I'm going then.'

'So go.'

'And I won't be coming back.'

'Boo bloody hoo.'

'You can only push me so far Moya.'

'I'm pushing. I'm pushing and you're still here.'

'I'm going.'

'Well bloody well go then.'

Dalglish, at the age of fifty, was more than ten years older than her. His problem was that he desperately wanted to marry her. Moya's problem was that she wanted to marry him, but on her own terms. She also wanted to continue rising through the ranks of the police force where she had just been promoted to the rank of inspector. Not bad for a former hippy wild-child and harassed single parent who had taken a five-year career break but was now secretly promising herself that she would become Big Mama Chief Constable one day. Dalglish wanted her to be a stay-at-home wife. He had his own haulage company. He could afford to keep her. She loved him dearly but she didn't want to be kept. So they fought bitterly, tearing lumps out of each other at every opportunity.

'What about our weekend in Paris?'

'What about it?'

'Are we still going this weekend?'

The holiday was already bought and paid for, half and half. They were due to fly out on Saturday morning. She had changed her shift, bought a new outfit, renewed her lapsed passport. She had been looking forward to it. Recklessness told her to tell Dalglish to shove his romantic weekend. Maturity lent her objectivity and told her to keep her options open. There was plenty of time to make up with him before Saturday but she couldn't admit that at the moment. He would be phoning her to apologize tomorrow morning. Nothing was more certain. It would be all right.

'Unless you've got somebody else to take,' she said.

'I might have.'

'I hope you'll be very happy together.'

Moya almost made the mistake of bursting out laughing at the ridiculousness of the situation but her stubborn pride strangled the sound and made it into a contemptuous grunt. She wanted Dalglish to stay. She wanted to sleep with him. Her sex drive was much more demanding than his. He knew it and used it as a weapon against her. She couldn't lose face by giving in to her hormones. She would just have to cut off her nose to spite her face. Humour faded rapidly to be replaced by anger at their mutual foolishness.

'Are you going or not?' she spat.

'I'm going.'

'Don't slam the door. You'll disturb the neighbours.'

'Fuck the neighbours.'

He went out and slammed the door. The coats hanging on the back of it billowed out dramatically and settled back. Moya stared for long minutes at the spot where Dalglish had been standing. She took a bread knife from the wall rack and threw it as hard as she could. It flew end over end across the kitchen and the point stuck deep into the door, quivering furiously. That made her feel a lot better.

# 7

The snake was out. Robert Ross touched the bulging s-shaped blue vein on his temple above the left eye and felt it pulse under the skin. He moved his hand and picked an irritating shred of tobacco from the corner of his mouth and rubbed it between the tough nicotine-stained skin of forefinger and thumb until it disappeared.

'It's not like the other islands on the loch. No, it's different is the Isle of Maree. The trees, the air, the atmosphere. There's something about it, something that sets it apart. You'll see for yourself tomorrow once we get out on the water.'

Ross studied his audience as he licked the edge of the cigarette paper and fashioned a thin roll-up. There were three of them, rich bastards with heavy-jowled faces, bulging stomachs and fat wallets. Some kind of diplomats attached to the European Commission in Brussels. They were smooth bastards as well, oozing the kind of arrogant self-confidence that made it a pleasure to ensure they got their feet wet. One was Greek with an unpronounceable name, another Belgian and the third English. They had come for the sea trout fishing, at its best in September, arriving too late that evening at the Lochside Hotel to get out on the water. They were now drinking after-dinner malts and chewing on big cigars in the Ghillies' Bar. They were big men, too big really for the small chairs at the oval tabole. They kept looking past Ross, over his shoulder and through the window at the loch where the rowing boats nuzzled at the jetty. Then their eyes would wander enviously to the big fish trophies on the walls, each privately hoping to hook at least as big a prize the next day. They kept drinking too, and buying drink for Ross. He didn't mind. He could take as much patronizing as they could dish out.

18

'I can hardly wait,' said Ralph Barrington, the English rich bastard who was the most excitable of the trio.

Ross rubbed the black and grey stubble on his chin with the back of his hand and replaced the lid on the tobacco tin. The Rizla packet went on the lid. He kept them waiting, scratching his head under the green woollen hat studded with colourful trout flies. On the fourth attempt he flicked a flame from his cheap novelty gas lighter, just as they all leaned forward offering the use of their fancy ones. One third of the roll-up disappeared instantly with just the faintest crackle of burning paper. Ross sucked in the smoke, enjoying his role as resident Ancient Mariner in the kingdom of fishermen. Another ghillie was giving another fishing party the same treatment a few tables along. Another was sitting at the bar in a head to head with a satisfied customer who had taken a twelve-pound beauty from the loch that afternoon.

Punters liked Ross and his stories, They expected it as part of the ghillie's job, and spinning his tall tales usually turned out to be worth a decent tip at the end of the week. From behind the bar the hotel owner, Fat Joe Hallett, winked at Ross in appreciation of another good performance.

'There's an ancient graveyard on the island you see and a ruined chapel.' Ross kept his voice low, making the clients strain towards him to hear properly. 'And in the graves there is a Viking prince and his princess. They both died young. Some say when he died in battle she killed herself so they could be buried together.'

'Vikings?' queried Barrington. 'What? Vikings here?'

Ross sat back and nodded wisely. He drained his whisky glass. The Greek took the hint and motioned to Hallett to bring another round.

'Oh yes. The Vikings sailed here from Scandinavia and occupied the islands in the loch. The local tribes couldn't get at them. Anyway it was all a very long time ago but some say the princess was never able to rest in peace. Some say her spirit drifts sadly round the loch to this day. They say you can see her if you look closely enough, all robed in white and almost invisible in the mist. That's what some say.'

19

'And have you seen her?' Barrington asked. His two companions looked at each other, grinned and leaned back simultaneously to blow cigar smoke at the ceiling.'

'Maybe. Maybe not. It's hard to tell when the mist is down on the water. You see movements on the islands and it's the deer. At least you assume it is the deer. Who knows.'

'Deer? On the islands?'

'That's right. There are twenty-seven islands, each one a little pristine patch of ancient pine forest, the kind that used to cover all of the Highlands. The stags come down from the mountains in the rutting season and swim across to do their business. I've seen some boats almost tipped over by swimming stags. At least one has been holed by antlers in my time. They had to use their jackets to plug the leaks to give them enough time to row back to shore.'

'You're joking,' Barrington said and his two companions laughed good-naturedly, leaning back to blow smoke at the ceiling.

Hallett delivered a tray of drinks. 'Our Robert never lies,' he said as he gathered in the empties. 'But like most fishermen he does have a tendency to exaggerate just a little.'

Ross shrugged to demonstrate his humility. 'Anyway, there's no deer on the Isle of Maree. Just the Viking graves and the wishing tree.'

'The wishing tree?'

'A very special tree. A holly tree. You hammer a coin into it, make a wish and it comes true.'

'I would wish to be able to see the princess,' Barrington said.

The Belgian's seat creaked loudly. He thumped his hand on the table. The glasses jumped and rattled. Ross snatched his up and emptied it in a single gulp to make it safe.

'I bet everybody wishes for the biggest sea trout ever caught,' the Belgian roared in his thick accent.

'It's not the wishing tree you consult if you want something like that,' Ross said. 'It's me.'

'Can you make my wish come true.'

'I can but try. And you don't even have to hammer coins into my flesh.'

'No?' The Belgian frowned. 'What do we have to do?'

'Pour whisky down my throat.'

The Belgian laughed and punched Barrington playfully in the shoulder. The Greek raised his arm to call for another round. Ross opened his tobacco tin but then accepted a fat cigar instead. He puffed at it and, one eye closed by the rising smoke, kept making roll-ups to pack into the tin for the next day.

He had got the taste for the drink now. He tapped the throbbing vein on his temple by way of casual salute. The snake was out. There was no holding it back.

# 8

*Wednesday, 23.06*

Silvery drops of water, illuminated by the moonlight, trailed from the blades of the oars as they dipped in and out of the calm water. The rowing boat made steady progress across the loch. Every few minutes the rower raised the oars high and looked round, holding back the fur-lined rim of an anorak hood and peering ahead over the water, checking the positions of the heavily wooded islands. Then the oars were lowered into the water for the next pull.

A couple of hundred yards away from one of the islands the head of the boat bumped against a flat rock that was barely visible on the surface of the loch. The rower stood up and jumped on to the rock, grabbing the prow and hauling it up just far enough to stop it floating freely.

Laura's body was lying on the bottom of the boat beside the transom at the stern. The rower clambered across to collect her, lifting her dead weight easily with an arm round the shoulders and another under the knees. Laura had been carried in the same manner from the whitewashed cottage, curled up like a little child in a parent's embrace, down to the wooden jetty to be placed in the boat.

Now the rower walked with elaborate care, high-stepping over the central seat and over the side of the boat in a strange makeshift funeral march.

On the rock platform the rower laid Laura down gently and arranged her arms and legs in a decorous sleeping position before kneeling beside her in an attitude of prayer, head bowed. Tears glistened on a face hidden in the depths of the hood. A voice broken by emotion tried to speak but the words would not come out properly formed. Instead, the rower took a small piece of paper from the anorak pocket and pushed into Laura's hand, closing her dead fingers tightly round it.

The rower remained motionless for a few minutes looking up at the incomplete white disc of the moon before turning to the boat. It slid back easily into the water and the oars swiftly moved into rhythmic motion, pushing it away. The face of the rower hidden in the folds of the hood never once left the white bundle on the rock as it merged into the distance and the darkness. Silvery drops of water trailed from the blades of the oars, marking the line of the return journey to where another waited at the cottage by the edge of the loch.

# 9

*Wednesday, 23.55*

David Fyfe heard Sally coming from a long way off. He was sitting in the new conservatory at the back of their house in the Border country south of Edinburgh. He put his feet against the low table and tilted the cane chair back to look up through the roof at the three-quarter moon floating in a shifting halo of ragged cloud.

'What's the matter darling? Can't sleep?'

'I tried not to waken you when I got out of bed.'

'Your absence wakened me.'

'Sorry.'

'What are you looking at?'

'The moon.'

He was inexplicably restless and unable to sleep. His brain wouldn't turn off. Thoughts raced around in it at random in a form of mental hyperventilation. He kept thinking he was about to shape his thoughts into something significant when meaning eluded him entirely. It was like driving into a snowstorm. The oncoming snowflakes came hurtling towards the windscreen but flew on past at the last instant, and you just kept on driving through this endless, formless tunnel.

Before Sally had come down to join him he had been staring obsessively at the garden shed. It was an ordinary wooden shed with a cracked side-window and planks of wood beginning to rot at the bottom. But inside it was stored his ill-gotten gains from the Angela Simpson episode. His old flame Angela, whom he had let walk away from a murder charge while helping himself to half her cash as a reward. Three hundred and sixty-eight thousand pounds was stuffed into old biscuit tins which were hidden in a specially dug hole under the floorboards. Not a soul suspected that he, a respected detective chief inspector of police, was a common thief. His past record made interesting reading. But what worried Fyfe most was that it didn't worry him at all.

He had intended the shed to act as a temporary hiding place while he set up various bank and building society accounts to take it but in the end he had decided just to leave it there. He didn't want anything written down, no records of accounts and balances. He didn't want anyone else to know of its existence. It made him a man of independent means, wonderfully solvent, with the conservatory, all-round double glazing, a Volvo estate in hideous metallic purple and a telephone credit account with Ladbrokes to show for it. He had yet to make a significant dent in the cash.

A very faint impression of guilt about his actions was imprinted on his mind like an after-image on a retina. Sally didn't know about the money. He hadn't told her about Angela either. She might understand one but not the other. She thought the conservatory was being paid for by instalments. She thought the purple Volvo with its fancy mobile phone belonged to the police force. Well, no one would voluntarily buy a car that horrible colour, would they? It was his only obvious indulgence. Otherwise he was happy to live frugally and take out his biscuit boxes from time to time to gloat miser-like over the thick sheafs of bank notes. It was tremendously liberating to be independently wealthy.

'What are you thinking?' Sally asked.

'I'm trying not to.'

Sally sat down beside him and let her hand rest on his leg. He looked right through the pair of them reflected in the glass of the roof and thought how Sally had been an ever-present in his life. They had been at school together, married young, become parents before they knew where they were. Then over the years they had drifted apart, had affairs, got divorced, and finally come together again as much friends as lovers. They had come full circle except that, since they weren't dead yet, the lines were presumably still being drawn.

Sally was totally recovered from her long drawn-out bout of depression and had got her old job back teaching Russian at the university. It was him that was depressed now, but they were sleeping together, eating together, talking together and going for walks on the hill together. It was almost like being newly-weds again. One of these days he really would ask her to marry him again.

He glanced sideways at her, admiring the familiarly cute kiss-curls on her forehead. His main concern was that if he was keeping such big secrets from Sally, what was it that she was hiding from him?

They sat staring up at the moon. The clouds were slowly obscuring it, like snow piling up in a drift. Finally it was gone and the countryside around the house was doused in total blackness. It was impossible to see the garden shed outside, impossible to see anything beyond his own transparent reflection in the glass.

'Come to bed now,' Sally ordered. 'It's after midnight.'

His mind was quieter now. His thoughts more lethargic. The snowstorm was over. He followed her up.

# 10

The shroud of impenetrable mist was beginning to burn off the surface of the water. It retreated ahead of the boat at a faster rate than the hollow puttering of the small outboard motor could match. Visibility lengthened from five yards, to ten, then fifteen, over the glass-calm surface of Loch Maree.

At the boat's stern Robert Ross tucked the arm of the outboard motor under his oxter and drew deeply on a freshly rolled cigarette protected by his cupped palm. The infusion of raw tobacco smoke mixed with the icily cold air raked his lungs and made him cough harshly.

It had been a long night in the bar and it seemed to him that he had barely curled up in his warm bed in the wooden chalet at the back of the hotel before Ralph Barrington came hammering at the door demanding to be ferried out into the early morning mist. Back in the hotel his two rich bastard companions, the Belgian and the Greek, snored on.

It was his own fault, Ross reasoned, for spinning his stock tales of swimming stags and ghostly Vikings. Barrington was impressed and gagging to get out on the loch, up at the crack of dawn and promising a tip of more than twenty pounds. He was desperate to have the chance to see the sites of these magical events for himself. The customer was always right, so Ross was obliged to drag himself out of bed, shake off the worst of a vicious hangover, and get a boat ready to take his client sailing before breakfast.

Land could be seen on both sides now, heavily wooded and flat to the left, a rock face rising into the mist to the right. At the head of the boat Barrington in his tartan shirt and bulky body-warmer was leaning forward like an overweight pointer dog, nose into the air, eyes weeping wind-bled tears. He was smiling beatifically.

Ross sniffed, coughed, shook his head, and spat shreds of tobacco over the side into the opaque black loch. He scooped up a handful of water. It was crystal clear. He sipped it from the hollow of his palm and it slid down his dry throat like melting ice.

The mist stopped retreating and kept its distance. The boat sailed inside its fixed boundaries, sending long whiskers of bow wave to stroke both shores.

'Will we see anything, Robert?' Barrington asked excitedly.

'Who knows?' Ross stifled a yawn. 'We might be lucky. It's the right time. Keep your eyes peeled.'

'What's that?'

Barrington stiffened and leaned even further forward. The boat rocked slightly as he shifted position. Somewhere ahead in the mist there was the faint sound of movement through undergrowth. A few seconds later it was followed by a ripely unpleasant smell.

'Is it a stag?' His voice had risen an octave with the excitement. 'Is it a stag? Is it?'

'It's a wild goat. There's a big herd of them on Letterewe Estate on the north side. You can smell the buggers a mile downwind.'

'It's absolutely horrible. What a stench.'

'If you're a goat you probably think it's lovely.'

'Chanel number five you mean.'

'More like camel number five.'

Ross swung the boat to the left and with his free hand picked another ready-made roll-up from the tin held between his legs. They had already passed the Isle of Maree. He would circle round and get it next time, once he was fully awake. He aimed for the channel between two half-formed islands as they emerged evenly from under the grey blanket. Their edges pressed in on the boat as it entered the narrows. The smell of the unseen goat quickly faded. Ross chuckled silently at Barrington's bulky figure hunched in front of him. A sucker for the ghost stories Barrington had been and, with the snake out, it had been a virtuoso performance by Ross. It only backfired when the man banged on his door wanting to go stag and ghost hunting when all sensible people were fast asleep.

Ross had been counting on a long lie. A ghillie's hours were long enough without adding to them unnecessarily. In ten years, coming to the job late at the age of thirty-six to escape the insurance industry and a looming nervous breakdown, Ross had never seen a single swimming stag or a floating ghost. But he couldn't admit that. He had to keep the punters happy. He had to make a living.

'What's that? Out there.'

Barrington was pointing ahead and looking back. His cheeks and nose glowed shocking pink. The tears were pooling in the creases around his eyes. Ross looked round him, trying to make sense of the solid shadows gradually forming from the grey haze. There was something ahead, something fluttering in the breeze like gala-day flags.

Ross rubbed his eyes and blinked. He half rose to better see past Barrington. The boat rocked slightly. The only noise was the metallic beat of the motor and the tinkling of the water against the hull. The mist stubbornly obscured the shape as the boat approached Parliament Rock, a large low-lying slab of stone in the loch where legend said Viking chiefs held their councils of war. It was hardly noticeable from a distance, even on a clear day. The rock rose no more than a few inches above the surface and was often submerged when the feeder rivers were in spate and the water was high.

The boat was less than twenty yards from it when the mist seemed to spontaneously part, like curtains being swept aside. Directly ahead the figure of a woman lying on her side was revealed.

'Is it a princess?' Barrington asked. 'Is it a Viking princess?'

Ross didn't reply. He stared open-mouthed. He saw the bare feet, the transparent white dress rippling over her, the curve of a hip, the long elegant fingers poised as if to conduct music, and the mass of black hair obscuring her face.

'Is she asleep?' Barrington asked.

He looked back at Ross and his eyebrows arched in mock amazement. Ross couldn't understand why Barrington was grinning so inanely. He looked from the Englishman's florid face to the motionless body and back again. He saw bright red cheeks on the Englishman and shiny black blood on the rock, reflecting the colourless dawn light that was pouring into the

27

world all around them. The blood puddled in a cushion under her head and fanned out. Black slowly turned to pale grey as he stared at it and the sun clawed its way through the mist. It wasn't blood at all, he realized. It was overlapping spirals of lichen growing on the rock.

'What a beautiful Viking princess you have here,' Barrington said.

A deep sense of foreboding paralysed Ross. He stood in the stern and could not move. The water beneath him could have been an empty space he was falling into. He watched as the bows struck the rock at an acute angle. There was a loud scraping noise. Both men were knocked off balance and ended in a heap in the bottom of the boat. The outboard motor raced as the boat turned lengthways and the propeller lifted clear of the water. Barrington scrambled to his feet and fell again. He was shouting something but Ross could not hear because of the whirling blades as they struck screeching sparks off the flinty hardness of the smooth rock.


# 11


*Thursday, 07.20*


David Fyfe rolled on to his back in the warm bed and enjoyed the taste of the farewell kiss that was planted softly on his lips.

'Are you going in to work today?' Sally asked.

'I might,' he said. 'I was going to take the afternoon off.'

'Don't overstretch yourself, will you?'

'I won't,' he replied, ignoring the heavy sarcasm.

'You need a shave.'

'Consider it done.'

'Are you looking after the dogs?'

'They can look after me.'

'What have they done to deserve such a fate?'

She kissed him again. Fyfe opened his eyes and closed them again immediately as the curtains were drawn back to let in an avalanche of bright daylight. Through half-shut eyes he was able to make out Sally blowing another kiss from the bedroom door. Then she turned away and was gone in a swishing curve of long coat and long hair. He listened to the sound of her footsteps going downstairs, the thump of the door, the car engine labouring to start and the cheery toot of the horn on departure. The silence afterwards was embroidered round the edges with birdsong.

I give it ten seconds, he thought, and began to count down by patting the covers. The rumble came rolling up the stairs by the time he reached six, across the landing by eight, and on the tenth beat exactly a black shape shot across the floor and jumped onto his chest. Fyfe was braced for it but still cried out in surprise when the black labrador bitch hit his stomach and almost winded him.

'Number Five, you beautiful black beast,' he said, grabbing her by the ears and rocking her head from side to side. 'Thanks for the alarm call. Now get off me.'

He pushed her off the side of the bed so that she fell on top of the other black labrador bitch sitting there. They were virtually identical apart from the grey hairs round the muzzle of the older dog. 'Sorry Jill, but you should learn to control your children,' Fyfe said.

Number Five, the runt of Jill's litter that he hadn't had the heart to part with, playfully pretended to bite her mother, who stoically ignored her. Fyfe stepped over the pair of them and went to the wash-hand basin in the corner. The dark shadow of the stubble growth on his chin made him look like a cartoon criminal. He splashed cold water in his face to kick-start the day and then scooped a couple of handfuls over the dogs. Number Five barked noisily and scrambled out of the way. Jill just looked up at him with sad eyes and twisted round to lick herself dry.

Fyfe was in a good mood. The world was a pleasant place. In the inside pocket of his suit jacket was his resignation letter, carefully phrased around mysterious and unspecified personal reasons. That would get them wondering. He liked the touch of intrigue and intended to offer no other explanation. The letter was kept in an unsealed envelope so that when the moment came he could write in the date and slap it down. The moment had to be right. When it came he would recognize it and savour it. Meanwhile, he was enjoying his life as it was and the envelope was getting ragged at the edges.

He dressed and checked the letter was in his pocket. He took it out and kissed it. He held it up to the light to see if he could read it through the envelope. Maybe today would be the day he would make his move. Maybe. Maybe not. For him, it was spiritually uplifting to have the option.

The phone rang while he was pulling on his trousers. Sally had already activated the answering machine. It cut in before he could get to it. He waited to see if it was anybody he wanted to talk to but whoever it was hung up when they heard the tape being triggered.

Fyfe frowned. He shifted the machine onto divert so the calls would follow him in the car. For some reason he interpreted the morning's first incoming call as a bad omen. It shattered his optimistic mood. Things couldn't keep going so well for him. Something had already happened and the consequences were out there waiting to mess him up. He was heading for a fall. Nothing surer.

'Come on, dogs,' he shouted, unnecessarily because they were sitting at his feet. 'Let's see what the big city has in store for us today.'

# 12

*Thursday, 07.28*

Eddie Illingworth could see his giant hourglass through the small gap in the bedcovers he had pulled over his head. It was surrounded by discarded clothes and shoes and empty beer cans. A pair of pink boxer shorts illustrated with flying pigs hung from one of the pillar supports. The top bulb, covered in little stickers given away free with breakfast cereal packets, was still almost full. The fine sand trickling through had created little more than a shadow in the bottom bulb. Twelve hours gone, he thought dreamily. Three and a half more days of his drinking binge to go.

The whining had woken him. It was a rhythmic keening that tore through his alcohol-sodden consciousness and demanded his attention. He pushed the bedcovers from his face and listened more carefully. The sound seemed to make the air around him vibrate. He sighed and frowned and shivered. Big sister Norma was having one of her fits. He had better check she was all right.

She had given him the room in her flat on a temporary basis while he sorted himself. That had been almost two years ago and Illingworth had no real intention of shifting himself. The arrangement was convenient, and the flat big enough for them not to get under each other's feet. They worked together at the office and then went their separate ways. More often than not Norma stayed elsewhere at night, presumably with one lover or another. She had a steady stream of them. Little brother Eddie didn't feel it was his place to ask and she didn't volunteer the information. She was a big girl and could take care of herself. She didn't charge him rent either. He wasn't going to crap in his own nest.

Illingworth opened Norma's bedroom door reluctantly. He had been vaguely aware of her arriving home at a ridiculous time in the morning and banging about the flat, but he couldn't be sure he hadn't just imagined it. But she was there in the bedroom. There was no doubting that because as the door swung back the whine, like a wounded animal suffering intolerable pain, increased in volume. Norma was on her knees on top of the bed. She was motionless with her hands clutched tightly between her legs and her head bowed. She had torn her nightdress and scratched her breasts and stomach. In the doorway Illingworth almost choked on a throatful of saliva. His heart thumped painfully, making him worry needlessly that the long dissolved stitches from his by-pass operation would burst open, little intrusive shreds of blue in a torrent of red pouring from his chest.

He hated it when Norma got like this. Thankfully, it wasn't a regular occurrence. In fact, this was the first time he remem-

31

bered it happening since he had set up residence in the flat. But whenever she succumbed it took him right back to his childhood and that first terrifying night when he was ten years old and his sister went mad.

Norma was fourteen then. She had been in her bedroom all evening, sulking because she had not been allowed to go on a school outing to the theatre. The whining was an unexpected, alien intrusion into the house. His mother had thought it was a gas leak or something but it didn't take long to follow the sound to the bedroom and find Norma kneeling on the bed. She was resting on her elbows with her backside in the air. Her night-dress was torn and there were scratches round her neck. As soon as her mother touched her the whining stopped.

'Michelle's hurt,' Norma said, looking up with unseeing eyes. 'Michelle's lying in the road. There's blood.'

Illingworth had stood in the doorway watching his mother comfort Norma and coax her back under the sheets and back to sleep. He was told she was having a bad dream. The next day Norma remembered nothing of what she had said. Later, they heard about the accident on the return trip from the theatre. Michelle was Norma's best friend at school. She was two months in traction recovering from her injuries.

There had been other times, most notably when she sensed the death of their father who was in hospital recovering from a heart attack. The ward sister phoned fifteen minutes after Norma's announcement. But more frequently her visions were obscure and apparently meaningless. Bad dreams, sceptics would call them. A couple of lucky hits from simple short-circuits in her brain didn't mean she could really see into the future. The educational psychologists had never found anything wrong with her. They put it down to her dependent and quixotic personality. Illingworth was a sceptic too, except he knew better.

So here he was again, standing in a doorway with his sister bent over on all fours on a bed, whining mournfully. She was a few inches taller than him, and a few inches wider all over. When they were children he had always been jealous of her for being bigger and stronger than him. It wasn't fair. She had been jealous of him for being daintier and more small-boned than

32

her. His hair was longer than hers. The family resemblance could be seen in their faces.

He stepped forward and touched her gently on the shoulder. The sound stopped abruptly. Her head swivelled round but her tear-damp eyes stared right through him. He felt the familiar icy chill at the base of his spine. It flowered outwards across his back like a frost pattern on a window pane. Having a psychic sister was fun as long as it wasn't taken seriously and the paranormal was confined to loopy stories on the glossy pages of the magazine he edited. This close up it scared the shit out of him.

'She's dead,' Norma whispered. 'Very dead.'

'Who's dead, Norma?'

Illingworth held her by the shoulders and tried to make eye contact but there was no connection there. She could hear him though. Her head cocked curiously at the sound of his voice.

'Can't see. I can't see. She's face down.'

'Where?'

'Water all round but she's floating. The fish are eating her.'

'Who is it?'

'Can't see.'

'Do you recognize her?'

'I'm not sure.'

Norma subsided slowly. Her eyes closed and her whole body relaxed. Illingworth eased her back down onto the bed and covered her up. She was sound asleep now. He knew she would remember nothing when she woke. He wouldn't tell her. It would only upset her.

He stood over her for a while, wondering if there really was somebody drowning, and where. There was nothing he could do about it anyway. The build-up of psychic energy, or whatever it was, had dispersed. The bedroom was warm not cold. The stiff frost pattern on his back had melted into cloying dampness. Illingworth listened to his heart slowing to a more sedate pace.

Norma's large frame looked incongruously delicate curled up in the foetus position with her sweat-damp hair on the pillow. A flutter of sibling love inspired him to lean over and kiss her forehead. He did love her hugely although it wasn't something

33

he would ever admit to her. It was an innate thing, a genetic transfer he couldn't alter. He didn't know what he would do without her. He got a wet cloth and washed the superficial scratches she had inflicted on herself before going to get himself a can of beer for breakfast. Still three and a half days to go.


# 13


*Thursday, 07.39*


Moya McBain sprinted the final one hundred metres to her back door and checked the time on her wristwatch. Twenty-two minutes and four seconds for the three-mile course. Not bad. A reduction of more than thirty seconds over three months. Add to that the loss of eight pounds and the new-found fascination with physical fitness triggered by the inevitability of her fortieth birthday was paying big dividends. She felt better. She looked better. She wanted it to last.

Her daughter Isabel was seated at the kitchen table, hurriedly spooning cornflakes into her face and brushing her hair at the same time. Moya tried to say good morning but there was not enough air in her lungs. Her legs were very tired as well and she was suddenly dizzy. She had to sit down.

'It's not good for you, mum,' Isabel said with her mouth full of cornflakes, speaking over the wallpaper music on the radio. 'This health kick you're on is downright dangerous. Life's short enough without wasting your time running round in circles.'

Moya tried to speak but couldn't. She smiled weakly instead and accepted the glass of orange juice Isabel pushed in her direction. It was ice cold. She could feel its coldness spreading down into the centre of her body and then flowing quickly out to the extremities.

'You should be taking things easier at your age, mum. Wild nights out with your fancy man followed by cross-country runs. I worry about you. Who's going to pay for me to get through university if you drop dead from a heart attack?'

'Don't worry, dear daughter,' Moya managed to say. 'I'm well insured.'

'Oh well, that's all right then.'

Isabel was up and away, shouting 'See you later' from the doorway. She looped a scarf round her neck. The coats on the back of the door billowed out and settled back as they had done when Ian Dalglish had left in the huff the previous night. Moya stared at the space where her sixteen-year-old daughter had been and wondered morosely if she was sleeping with her boyfriend yet. If she was, it was more than her mother was doing with hers.

Moya wanted to ask Isabel but was afraid to hear the answer. Her only baby had grown up into an attractive and intelligent young woman, very much like herself. Innocence was so soon gone. The girl should have been more suspicious of men since she knew the whole story about her long-lost father doing a runner at the first hint of pregnancy. But she wasn't. She wouldn't be told. Isabel would learn the hard way. Like mother, like daughter.

Moya sighed and rose to her feet, kicking off her trainers. The muscles had tightened in her thighs and she walked stiff-legged up the stairs to the bathroom. She dumped the track-suit top and trousers in the laundry basket. The plain T-shirt was soaked in sweat and sticking to her breasts and stomach. The shorts were skimpy on top of a slim pair of legs. Her short hair was unkempt and spikey. She would have looked several years younger than her age if it had not been for the heavy bags under her eyes. They piled on the years. The more she worried about them and tried to get rid of them, the less she was able to sleep and the worse they seemed to get.

She switched on the shower and adjusted the heat of the water. She stepped out of the shorts and was pulling the T-shirt over her head when the phone rang. Hopefully it would be Ian and they could begin the ritual process of making up. A little humility was a small price to pay for a weekend in Paris. Knowing the house was empty she went naked into the bed-room to answer the phone. A pleasantly cool draught wrapped itself round her as she sat on the edge of the bed. Downstairs she could just make out the sound of the radio playing.

'Is that Inspector McBain?'

Moya recognized the deep male voice immediately. It wasn't Ian. It was George Rusling, assistant chief constable, and the man almost everybody believed she was sleeping with to win her fast-track promotion. She wasn't but she had no doubt he was willing, given half a chance. Rusling had decided he would help her career anyway, no strings attached. They had never spoken about it but he seemed to enjoy the rumours. A typical man, even if he was more likeable than most. He was a big pal of Ian's too, both of them committee members of the most exclusive golf club in town.

'Inspector McBain speaking.'

'Moya, are you dressed yet?'

She rubbed her breasts and enjoyed imagining him breaking out in a cold sweat. If only he could see her now, that would knock him out of his stride.

'Almost. Why?'

'I know you're not due on shift until the afternoon but if you were to get your pretty little behind in here fast you might learn something to your advantage.'

'Like what?'

'Like, a murder case is about to be allocated to the most senior investigating officer available only there isn't one available yet.'

'A murder.' She caught her breath and sat erect. 'You'll give it to me?'

'It looks like a juicy one too. A lady-in-the-lake mystery.'

'For me?'

'First come, first served Moya. This is your early-morning call. Don't let on I told you. Make the most of it.'

She put the phone down and forgot about the shower, rushing about the bedroom to find her clothes. She would have liked to progress through the ranks without Rusling's patronage but she was a realist, tough-minded enough to believe she would have got there eventually without his help. But every police force had its favourites and she was an easy target for inbred prejudice and not-so-veiled insults. She mustn't get paranoid, she told herself. An infiltrator in a man's world had to be mentally strong. Rusling's interest in her was coincidental, not crucial. Nobody got anywhere without being good at the job. She would beat the bastards off, and stay ahead of the game. Then she would be able to pick somebody from the lower ranks to patronize.

The trick was never to let them know about the turmoil of uncertainty going on inside, the fear of making a mistake no man would ever make, the fear of humiliation and ridicule. Never let them know about the lonely nights spent weeping into a pillow when she reverted to being the little girl the boys at school called Moaning Moya. By day, she never cried and she never let them see the doubts that persisted like a bad migraine.

Suicides were common in the Highlands, murders rare. It was early days. It might turn out to be a suicide so she shouldn't get her hopes up. She had never been in charge of a murder inquiry before but now the seasonal combination of holidays, sickness, and suspension through drink-driving had given her the opening and the opportunity to make her name. Superintendent Mark Ryder, her immediate superior, had already made it clear he didn't trust her on simple housebreakings, let alone murders. It was mutual distaste. They didn't get on. Whenever she was near him she was gripped by a wicked desire to grab his testicles and watch his eyes water when she squeezed with all her strength.

She had complained to George. He had pulled rank and got her name put in the frame for this case. Nothing wrong with getting a little help from a friend, except that Ryder would resent it hugely. It was up to her to show she could hack it.

Her pulse raced with restrained excitement at the prospect of taking charge of a murder case. She was fully dressed and presentable within two minutes. A quick tidy of her hair and straightening of seams. At the back door in three.

She hesitated for a moment, realizing that she was wearing the clothes she had bought for her romantic French weekend. She dismissed the idea that Rusling had deliberately given her the case to keep her and Ian apart.

'Sorry Ian,' she said regretfully to herself. 'Paris is off.'

# 14

The hot towels over David Fyfe's face sterilized the air he breathed in through his nostrils. He imagined it working like a strong drain cleaner, dissolving the accumulated debris inside his lungs, following the various u-bends to scour the veins and arteries through his heart, and flushing the synaptic junctions in his brain. Not a very scientific picture but a pleasing one that gave him the illusion of perfect health for a little while. It didn't last, of course. Thirty seconds at most then he was able to relax and breathe easily. His skin swiftly learned to tolerate the towels, originally so hot that their touch was almost unbearable.

The monthly shave in Sergio's basement barber's parlour had become another of the small rituals Fyfe liked to spread through his waking hours. He had been passing the red and white pole attached to the railings for years, always glancing down through the window at customers sitting in the big old-fashioned dentist-style chair. Mostly they were getting their hair cut but every now and then he would see a towel-wrapped head and the flash of an open razor in the hand of the white-smocked barber.

The parlour was below ground in a cluttered terrace of Chinese and Indian restaurants and shops with fruit and vegetables taking up half the pavement. By day the smell of bananas and oranges was dominant. By night curry and sweet-and-sour took over. Sergio was the barber, a man with huge hands and a Desperate Dan chin. He had a concave nose and an old scar on one cheekbone. The first time Fyfe lay back in the chair all soaped up and Sergio came at him with the razor a mild panic attack made him flinch nervously.

'Eet's a okay, Meester Fyfe,' said Sergio in an accent twenty years in Edinburgh had scarcely affected. 'Zere are two zings in life ve must learn to trust abzolutely. One iz our wife when she says she loves us and ze uzzer is ze barber wiz ze razor in hees hand.'

Fyfe learned to trust absolutely, no longer twitching when the blade scraped his throat. For such a big man, Sergio had a very light touch. He would chat away as he worked, occasionally bursting into song to accompany the Pavarotti tape that played endlessly. He would offer homilies and parables with the punch-line often lost in the tangle of his impenetrable English.

'Always remember Meester Fyfe, zat ze policeman's bottom eez never ze fattest.'

That couldn't be what he meant but it was how Fyfe interpreted it. The good thing about Sergio was that, because of the nature of his job, he never expected a reply.

Fyfe always allowed two days' growth of beard in preparation for Sergio. It was his Calvinist upbringing. If he was going to pay to be shaved, he wanted to make it worth his while. Afterwards the skin of his face felt impossibly smooth, like polished wood. It was a lovely sensation. Twenty-four hours later the faintest edge of roughness would have returned. Time marches on, he always thought stoically.

Below the total white-out of the rapidly cooling towel Fyfe heard his portable phone warble. The sound conveyed no intimation of doom this time, he noted. This call was going to be a welcome one. He retrieved the phone from his pocket and held it to his ear, pressing the receive button.

'David Fyfe.'

'Davie my boy, how are you? Mark Ryder in Inverness here.'

Fyfe had to think to place Ryder. It came quickly. Superintendent in the Highlands, low handicap golfer, kids into skiing and hill-walking, wife into bridge. They had been together for two weeks on a fraud investigation induction course. Ryder had an eye for the women and he liked a drink. Sound man.

'Mark. Superintendent now isn't it? What can I do for you?'

'Buy me that drink you owe me.'

'I'll start saving up now.'

'There is something else, naturally enough. You're the chosen one from the crime squad to help out on difficult inquiries.'

'Yeah. Got a difficult inquiry, have you?'

'Not yet, but it might go that way. I've formally requested your help and I've already squared it with your boss. He passed on your personal number. Can you get up here pronto?'

Fyfe liked the idea of a trip north into the Highlands. The dogs would appreciate it too. All that empty space to explore. He liked the idea of the spontaneity, the sudden adventure. He lifted the warm towel from his face and grinned at Sergio. The phone crackled. Pavarotti hit a high note.

'What's the problem?' Fyfe asked.

'We have a potential murder at Loch Maree. Know where that is?'

'I'll look it up on the map.'

'Wester Ross. Woman's body found by a fishing party but she's not the problem.'

'What is then?'

'Well, the powers-that-be have assigned a young female detective as officer in charge of the case and frankly I don't think she's up to it.'

'Oh dear, that's a bit politically incorrect, isn't it Mark?'

'Between you and me, Dave, she's only there because an assistant chief who must remain nameless has been inside her knickers, that and an epidemic of flu and holidays shoving her to the front. I think she'll make a hash of it. Nice legs but no brains, if you know what I mean.'

'You're not paranoid are you, Mark?'

'I wasn't till everybody started talking about me.'

'So you want me to babysit this floozie with a badge?'

'It has to be someone from outside, Dave. Office politics, you understand.'

'I reckon I can handle her, legs and all.'

'Good. Her name is Moya McBain. She'll be based at the Lochside Hotel on Loch Maree. Where are you now?'

Fyfe looked at Sergio cleaning the razor in the sink. 'I'm in bed with my Italian lover.'

Sergio looked at him in the mirror, fluttered his eyelashes and snapped the razor shut.

'You should be so lucky,' Ryder said. 'Are you in Edinburgh?'

'It's a very romantic city.'

'Then it will take you four or five hours to get there. I'll tell her you'll be there late afternoon.'

'Have you told her how devastatingly good-looking I am?'

'I'll break it to her gently.'

'And I'll be gentle with her. I'm leaving now.'

Fyfe ended the call and decided he wouldn't hand in his resignation that day. A short sojourn in the Highlands showing the ropes to an attractive and ambitious female detective sounded like his kind of job. Maybe she would sleep with him to advance herself. It would keep him out of the office too so no-one could annoy him. He had known it was going to be a good call before he answered it. He had known today was not going to be the day to hand in his resignation. He heaved himself out of the chair. His palms over both cheeks confirmed the smoothness of his face.

Sergio flicked his razor shut. 'Ze bizness, Meester Fyfe,' he said, admiring his handiwork. 'You are once more a new man again.'

Fyfe flexed his jaw to get accustomed to the feel of the newly-mown skin. 'Same old one, I'm afraid, Sergio,' he replied.

# 15

*Thursday, 09.47*

Donald McIsaac, the local policeman at Gairloch for most of his adult life, could remember the last murder he had been involved in. He had just been installed in the police house, fresh from training college. He was newly married and the first child was on the way. He had still to wear the creases out of his uniform. His first official act was to attend a motor accident at Kerrysdale. Nobody hurt, not much damage. That was day one of his career. Day two was the murder.

The victim was a well-known local poacher, Sleekit Sam, found face down in a ditch with his hands tied behind him and the side of his head blown off. The vendetta between him and the gamekeeper on the estate was common knowledge. Geordie Sim was waiting in his gun room for McIsaac and the detective sent out from Inverness. When they arrived he was cleaning his shotgun, plunging the rod in and out of the barrel. They hesitated in the doorway but Geordie put down the gun and waved them in. They let him talk them through descriptions of the antlers and skulls that adorned the walls and when he had finished he held out his wrists for the handcuffs.

'I was going to frighten Sam,' he explained. 'Tied him to a tree and took aim. Stupid bastard didn't keep his head still.'

It was all settled between dawn and dusk. Geordie Sim went quietly, admitted everything, and was sentenced to life imprisonment. He served eight years and would have had his old job back except he couldn't get his firearms licence renewed. He was given a job as an estate worker and handled guns anyway. Two years later he dropped dead from a heart attack just as he was sighting on a big old stag down near Applecross. It was 1966, McIsaac remembered. A Saturday. The day England won the World Cup. A sad day for everyone.

Now McIsaac had a snow-white beard, two weeks to go to retirement and maybe around the same length of time before his first grandchild was born. When fat Joe had phoned him early that morning with news of the lady in the loch his first thought had been how a murder at each extremity of his career would make it beautifully symmetrical.

He had called in reinforcements and gone out in one of the hotel boats to see the body for himself. From a distance she seemed to float on the water, white robes fluttering about her, larger than life through the lenses of the binoculars. No obvious candidate as perpetrator this time. No obvious signs of the victim's identity. Too many strangers, too many second homes in the area. McIsaac peered at her from the boat. He didn't go ashore. He had no idea who she might be or how she had ended up on the rock.

In the hotel he sympathized with a morose Robert Ross, who assured him it had to be murder. She couldn't have battered herself to death and then swum out to the rock. McIsaac didn't doubt it.

And he listened patiently to the excitable Englishman apologizing for thinking initially it was all a stunt, a ghostly Viking princess laid out on the rock especially to impress him. He had thought it was all part of the holiday package. The Belgian and the Greek wanted guarantees that no names would appear in the newspapers. They seemed to think it was a diplomatic incident of great magnitude, not the murder itself but the fact that they were associated with it. McIsaac deflected all inquiries expertly, saying he had no authority and they would have to wait for senior officers.

And here came the senior officer in charge, a shapely young woman in a short skirt with just a trace of hesitation in her voice to betray her nervousness. Nice body, nice legs. A couple of plain-clothes sergeants stood behind her grinning inanely and giving the unsettling impression that they knew exactly what McIsaac was thinking. The forensic team arrived in their van. A team of navy divers from the Kyle base drew up with all their equipment. More uniformed officers followed in a mini-bus. Dr Albert Eames, the pathologist, appeared, unfolding himself out of a low-slung MG sports car and stalking off into the hotel.

The small car park was almost full. So much dust had been stirred up by the arrivals it stung McIsaac's eyes as he stood at the entrance explaining the situation to the delightfully long-legged DI McBain. This must be the modern way to investigate a murder, he was thinking. Last time it was just me and another man. I bet this lot don't beat our record.

'Thank you, Constable McIsaac,' the young woman was saying. 'Can I ask you to organize the boats. I want to get out to her and see for myself before we begin taking statements.'

# 16

*Thursday, 11.51*

Robert Ross waited in the first floor room they gave him to keep him apart. He sat at a table by the window with his hands pressed flat on the surface to stop them shaking when he wasn't rolling cigarettes. Normally he could do one in twenty seconds but since that morning he had been struggling to beat five minutes. Even then the roll-up was so loose it generally burned away after a couple of puffs and he had to start making a new one all over again.

Fat Joe provided a plate of sandwiches which Ross didn't want and a pot of coffee that left grains like thick mud in the bottom of the mug.

'I don't know if this scandal will be good or bad for business, Bobby,' he said. 'What do you think? The hotel will be in all the papers. Do you think I should buy some ads as well?'

Donald McIsaac got him more tobacco when he ran out and slipped him a hip flask of whisky to calm his nerves.

'Won't be long now,' McIsaac told him. 'The lassie'll be back to hear your story then we can let you loose in the bar.'

Ross didn't speak back to either of them. He drank coffee and smoked and watched the policemen in their white nylon overalls board the boats and head out into the loch. Parliament Rock was visible from the end of the jetty but not from the hotel window. From where he sat a jutting tree-covered headland screened it from view. The day was clear and still. The joins between land and water and land and sky were smudged. Colonies of midges stained the air at the edges of the loch. The sun passed its midday peak, dragging the shadow on the weathered stone pedestal of the sundial in the little ornamental garden round from west to east.

Ross could see himself from the night before, the centre of attraction as he told his compelling tales of Viking princesses and swimming stags. The rapt faces, the jaws hanging slackly. He had them all on toast. And from the bar he was suddenly being knocked off his feet as the boat bumped into Parliament Rock and the propeller was chewing into it and striking sparks.

'I knew we would find her,' the Englishman kept saying, apparently thinking it was all one big joke. 'Our rendezvous here was ordained.'

In the seat by the window, a spasm of abstract terror seized Ross. The missing hours between the stories in the bar and the discovery in the loch were a total blank. He sucked at a roll-up.

44

The tobacco was burned in a single inhalation. Its crackling sounded inordinately loud to him.

At the rock he had shut off the petrol to the outboard motor to stop the racket. Then it wouldn't start again. Six times the motor coughed and died. Eventually he got the oars out and they began to row away. Barrington was babbling hysterically. He had realized it was all very true. She wasn't a dummy. She was very dead. It was not a joke for his benefit.

The boat slewed to one side because Barrington wasn't pulling hard enough on his oar. Ross shouted at him. His next stroke skimmed the surface and he overbalanced, landing on his back with his feet sticking up. Once he struggled back into a seated position, almost capsizing the boat, the woman and the rock vanished into the mist.

By the time they reached the shore Barrington had subsided from rambling incoherence to disconcerting silence. Ross wished he had stayed in bed, left the woman for somebody else to find. He was remembering now, piecing together what had happened. It had not been a dream after all. It hadn't happened inside his head but outside it. He began to see the funny side. 'But apart from that, Mr Barrington, how have you enjoyed your holiday so far?'

In the hotel only Raymond, the chef, and Miranda, the breakfast waitress, were awake. They didn't believe him when he tried to explain. They looked at each other over a pot of scrambled eggs and shook their heads. Fat Joe appeared, scratching hard at the sides of his overhanging belly. He sneered and ostentatiously smelled Ross's breath. Then Barrington came into the kitchen. 'It's all true,' he said quietly.

The customer is always right. Raymond wiped his hands on his apron and went to call the police.

In the next thirty minutes the imperceptibly rising wind dispersed the mist, shooing it away like a teacher emptying the playground of children when the bell rings. Fat Joe got a pair of binoculars and waddled out to the end of the jetty with Raymond, Miranda and a group of curious, half-awake guests. 'Fuck me sideways,' he said, handing the binoculars on. 'It is true. She's lying there like last week's washing. Any idea who she is?'

Ross shook his head in reply and bit the inside of his lip. 'She's not a Viking princess, that's for sure,' Barrington said.

Loch Maree was placid and calm in the early afternoon. The reflection of the mountainous north shore went as deeply down into the water as its rocky reality climbed into the sky above. The sound of an outboard approaching the jetty droned lazily across the water. At the end of the jetty the navy divers were relieving the boredom by swimming. From the first-floor window Ross watched as a boat berthed and the young woman detective who had asked him to wait in the room made her awkward way ashore. He had mentally prepared the statement he would give to the police. McIsaac came in to check on him.

'You'll be first Bob. She'll want you down in the office.'

Ross rose obediently and then sat down. McIsaac offered the hip flask again. Ross shook his head. He didn't want to drink too much.

He wanted to make sure they believed him when he told them his story. Verisimilitude was required. This time he was confident he could convince them his story was true.

# 17

*Thursday, 13.23*

Moya McBain was sure her skirt was too short. It was a mistake. It might have been sophisticated and glamorous on the chic streets of Paris, but in a rowing boat heading out to view a murder victim on a rock in the middle of a loch it was only inconvenient. Everyone had tried hard not to stare at her legs, a sure sign that she was showing too much, and she could imagine their condescending smiles behind her back. She resisted the temptation to adjust her skirt. There was just no space to do it demurely in the boat with her knees up to her chest.

On the rock she had been unable to go down to inspect the neck bruising properly. Dr Eames was crouching over the body, his balding head below the hemline of her skirt. He had looked up and been momentarily flummoxed by the sight of her thigh at the end of his nose. He took off his glasses and cleaned them to hide his embarrassment as he stood up. He was a tall man, well over six feet, even with a pronounced stoop. She was glad she hadn't worn anything low cut or his nose would have been pointing down her cleavage.

'Looks like a single blow to the side of the head with a blunt instrument,' he said. 'Then strangulation, probably while she was unconscious. There is no sign of any blood or tissue under the fingernails so she didn't fight back against her attacker. Of course that's assuming there was only one. Somebody could have held her hands behind her back, but I doubt it.'

'She didn't fall then?' Moya asked, aware of the ridiculousness of the question as it came out.

'Not on this rock she didn't,' Eames said, replacing his glasses and looking round. 'And she's been dead a fair while too. Probably a day, maybe longer.'

There was not enough space on the rock for everybody. Three boats were floating alongside it. Two were full of officers in regulation overalls waiting to be told where to search, and the other accommodated the forensic team with all their boxes and bags. It had already disembarked a photographer who was flashing away at the corpse.

'She was killed elsewhere then and dumped out here,' Moya said.

'I would say so,' Eames conceded, trying hard not to look at her legs but failing. 'As clear a case of strangulation as you can get. Somehow I don't think she was persuaded to come dancing out here. She was dead on arrival.'

'Pretty strange.'

'People do the strangest things.'

'Pretty bizarre in fact.'

Eames crouched down again and reached out to touch the slightly blood-crusted hair. 'Woman in white. The lady of the lake. The headline writers will have a field-day on this one.'

It was only then, standing on Parliament Rock in the middle of the loch, that she fully appreciated her luck. This was no ordinary murder, certainly not a domestic dispute with kitchen knives within convenient reach. This was very different. Her pulse raced with repressed excitement. A semi-naked female body dumped in an almost inaccessible location but one where it was certain to be discovered. A practical mind, if not an entirely rational one, had done this. If she could crack the case she would make her name once and for all. Sour-faced Super-intendent Ryder, who wouldn't have put her on the simplest housebreaking if he had his way, would have to say well done. Nobody would laugh behind her back then.

'One other thing before you go,' Eames said.

He was crouching down again and was cradling the dead woman's hand in his. With a pair of tweezers he carefully extracted a crumpled bit of paper from the fist. He used his free hand to snap open a clear plastic bag to take it.

'What is it?' Moya asked.

'It was inserted after death. The fingers were already in a state of rigor mortis when it was pushed in.'

'What does it say?'

Eames peered closely. He adjusted his glasses and shook his head. 'See if you can make it out.'

Moya took the bag and had it logged and recorded as evidence. The paper was roughly four inches square. It had been torn off a pad or a notebook. Three edges were straight, the other ragged. The writing was a scrawl but easily legible. *Laura, please forgive me*, it said. It was signed *Bobby*.

The tail of the final letter was cut short where the paper had been torn off at the bottom.

# 18

*Thursday, 15.35*

The short skirt was still a problem in the boat on the way back to the hotel. Moya tried to reimpose her authority, issuing instructions to the two squad detective sergeants, Charlie Simpson and Peter McCue, who had driven up in the same car with her from Inverness. She did it sitting in the bows, talking back over her shoulder so that she wasn't showing too much leg. They were the kind who played stupid chauvinistic games, the kind who huddled in a locker room corner and laughed amongst themselves.

But it didn't matter. She had done all the routine scene of crime stuff. Everything was ticking over. She kept going over the investigation strategy in her head. Nothing missed. No gaps. Nothing left to chance. She would show them. Over and over again she read the message on the little bit of paper inside its protective plastic bag. It was obvious who Laura was. She had to find out about this Bobby. Simple really.

No more short skirts, she promised herself, as she was helped ashore at the hotel jetty. She grabbed hold of McIsaac's arm to steady herself. He had a kindly face, careworn and deeply creased behind the white beard. It was reminiscent of her father, long dead but not forgotten. She walked alongside him on the wooden slats of the jetty, careful not to get her heels stuck in the narrow spacings.

'The bloody European threesome are kicking up a fuss, Ma'am,' McIsaac said. 'They're worried they're going to be caught up in some kind of sex scandal.'

'What makes them think this is a sex scandal?'

'A crime of passion, they're saying. It has to be if there's a woman involved. And they want away before the media circus begins.'

'They can't go yet.'

'That's what I told them. They don't like it.'

'Then they can lump it.'

McIsaac was enjoying himself. 'They tried to claim some kind of diplomatic immunity,' he said. 'Made out that because they were big cheeses from Brussels, but I told them they would have to wait anyway.'

'Good,' Moya confirmed. 'Fishermen should know how to be patient. Are any of them called Robert?'

'I don't know Ma'am. I don't think so. Why?'

'Can you find out?'

'Of course.'

Moya stopped beside the sundial in the ornamental garden in

front of the hotel and tried to work out what time it was from the position of the shadow on the weathered stone. The lower half of the pedestal was covered in a yellow-green moss.

'It's just after half past three, Ma'am,' McIsaac told her.

'Thanks. My daughter has run off with my watch.'

'You should get the police on her.'

McIsaac explained that he had requisitioned the hotel office for her to work from. He had got a copy of the voters' roll from the sub-post office at Gairloch and a copy of the council tax register showing properties and their owners in the parish. 'A good few hundred round the loch,' he said. 'People like to hide away in remote nooks and crannies up here.'

Moya started to think through an investigation strategy. Every property would have to be visited, every owner contacted. They would begin with those on the south shore closest to Parliament Rock. The most urgent requirement was to get an identity for the victim. McCue was delegated to head south with a set of fingerprints. There was jewellery too; a ring with a cryptic inscription and a locket that had yet to be prised open. It was only a matter of time before they got a name.

'Oh, before I forget. Superintendent Ryder phoned from Inverness to say that a Chief Inspector David Fyfe is heading north to help you.'

'What?' Moya tried not to let the news upset her. 'Who?'

'Fyfe his name is. Some big-shot detective from big-shot Edinburgh. Active liaison officer with Scottish Crime Squad, I think they call it. He's quite famous actually. He's been involved in a number of high profile cases.'

'Yes, I know. I have heard of him. I didn't think I would be meeting him here though.'

'Maybe you're just lucky that way.'

That bastard Ryder was deliberately trying to humiliate her, Moya thought. He couldn't just let her get on with it. The pity was that she had admired Fyfe's photograph in the papers, followed his career with interest and envy. At one point she had even considered writing a letter to him but had decided that would be too naff. She had always wondered what he would be like to meet face to face. Now circumstances meant

50

she would have to be cold and distant, rather than friendly and charming. She had no intention of handing over control of this case. It belonged to her. David bloody Fyfe wasn't going to take it away from her.

'Do I have a choice in this?' she asked angrily.

McIsaac shook his head, disclaiming responsibility. 'As I understand it DCI Fyfe comes up to look over your shoulder. If the case goes well he takes the credit. If it doesn't you take the blame.'

A man came round the side of the hotel and along the path into the garden. He was unshaven, wearing a tweed jacket and a colourful woollen hat. Moya realized as he approached that the colours were fishing flies on the dark wool. The man lifted the hat from his head and twisted it between his hands. Moya wondered how he could do that without getting the hooks caught in his skin. McIsaac stepped protectively in front of her.

'Here's a Robert for you,' McIsaac said. 'Robert Ross, the ghillie who found the body. Looks like he can't wait to be questioned.'

'Good afternoon, Mr Ross,' Moya said in her best authoritative voice. 'I'm just going inside. We'll get round to you soon enough.'

'No, no, your honour,' Ross said, side-stepping McIsaac and dropping a few inches onto the lawn. 'I need to tell you now.'

'Everybody will get their chance.'

'No point. No point.'

'What do you mean, Bob?' McIsaac asked.

'I can tell you who the murderer is.'

Moya did not know how to react to this unexpected announcement. His name was Robert. McIsaac had called him Bob. Others presumably would call him Bobby. Ross's shadow fell parallel to the one thrown by the pedestal of the sundial. She did not smile. She did not frown. Her first thought was that it couldn't be this easy. McIsaac spoke.

'What do you mean, Bob?' McIsaac asked again.

'I know who the murderer is,' he repeated.

'Who?' Moya asked impatiently.

If the pause was for dramatic effect it worked very effectively.

51

Moya was sure she saw the shadows creep round almost imperceptibly. Faces at the hotel windows stared down on them. The air around her fractured into a million flying insects.

'It was me,' Ross said proudly.

# 19

*Thursday, 15.56*

David Fyfe did not hurry on his way north. He passed the time by fantasizing about what Moya McBain might look like. He had a good feeling, a premonition that they would hit it off. He was barely over the Forth Bridge before they were in bed together.

He had a leisurely, greasy lunch at the Little Chef restaurant on the A9 south of Inverness and bought a map to plan his route the rest of the way to Loch Maree. As the roads got narrower and the terrain rougher he stopped frequently to appreciate the beauty of the Highland scenery and to let the two dogs run free. With any luck, the inquiry would be finished by the time he got there.

Leaning on the parapet of a picturesque hump-backed bridge over a rocky riverbed in the middle of nowhere he phoned Sally to tell her where he was and what was happening. Earlier he had ignored two incoming calls, guessing that it might be somebody telling him to turn back. He had no intention of doing that, even though there was nothing on the radio about any murder. If it was a false alarm he would find out for himself in due course while enjoying a pleasant drive in the country.

Fyfe saw the hotel from a long way out at the southern tip of the loch. It blinked in and out of sight on the undulating road as he was reeled in towards it and the heavily wooded islands that seemed to fill its back garden.

As he drew up in the car park a weary-looking police constable at the entrance pocketed a hip flask he had been drinking from and eyed him suspiciously. Jill and Number Five tumbled out of the car and began sniffing around. A long, curving conservatory on the front of the hotel was full of plant pots and whicker armchairs but devoid of people. A cloud of midges hovered around the hanging lamp above the door. It burned uselessly in the late afternoon light.

'Evening, constable,' Fyfe said. 'Seen any dead bodies around by any chance?'

'What do you know about that?' McIsaac replied suspiciously.

'Not a lot yet.' Fyfe looked up at the pale sky and through a scatter of trees across to the rounded black bulk of Slioch. 'Nice night for a murder hunt.'

McIsaac's eyes narrowed. 'Are you a reporter by any chance?'

'Well, I've been accused of many things in my time but never with being a member of Her Majesty's Press. Actually, it's a whole lot worse than that.'

'It is?'

'I'm a policeman.'

'Get away,' McIsaac mocked. 'So am I.'

Fyfe showed his identity card. 'Your friendly Scottish Crime Squad representative. I'm looking for DI McBain. She around?'

McIsaac had relaxed. He smiled as he stood aside. 'Oh yes, sir. The office is beside the dining room through the back. DI McBain will be expecting you. You're just a little late though.'

'I am? It's not even dark yet.'

'We've got somebody for the killing. He's making a full confession as we speak. Beat my record would you believe?'

Fyfe took in the information and tried not to show surprise. He scratched at his twitching eyebrows. 'You won't be needing me then,' he said. 'I'll just say hello and goodbye and go away again.'

'DI McBain's pretty pleased with herself.'

'I'm pleased with her too. I get to go on a lovely drive in the Highlands and I don't even have to work at the end of it. I'd like to shake that woman by the hand.'

'On you go, sir. You'll find everybody in the bar.'

Fyfe called to his dogs. 'I don't suppose they object to animals since it's a hunting/shooting/fishing hotel.'

'No more than they object to people,' McIsaac said, following on behind.

The deserted reception area had a rack of tourist brochures and a glass display case full of tartan cloth and cashmere sweaters. One wall was entirely covered in six-inch square, glass-fronted boxes containing different salmon and trout flies. Fyfe was drawn to the sound of voices off to his left. Above a door was the sign, Ghillies' Bar. The letters were burned into a rectangular piece of tree bark. He pushed the door open and found a small crowded room lined with stuffed fish and ten-foot rods. He thought one wall was a mural, then he realized it was a window looking out onto the still waters of the loch.

The talk stopped and most heads turned as he entered. Jill and Number Five sat on either side of him facing outwards like book-ends or bodyguards. McIsaac pushed past him and made a general introduction. The fat man behind the bar declared himself the owner and offered to shake hands from a ridiculous distance. He waved an arm at the room indicating estate workers and guests and a little covey of drafted-in police in blue overalls gathered round a table crowded with pint glasses of orange squash. At another table were four young men in wet suits and bare feet. McIsaac said he would go and announce Fyfe's arrival to Moya McBain.

'Can I get you a drink Chief Inspector?' Joe Hallett asked.

'Why not,' Fyfe said. 'It was a dusty journey up here. I need something to clear my throat. I'll take a pint of lager.'

Hallett started to pour it. 'We would never have thought it of our Robert. He was always a bit strange. I'll give you that. But I never thought he had the killing of somebody in him.'

'He did it, did he?'

'Looks that way. Broke down and confessed the moment DI McBain skewered him with her beautiful baby blues. Crime of passion, it was. Apparently there had been secret meetings in the woods. Our Robert? Who would have thought it of him?'

'Is that him?'

Fyfe nodded at the row of half a dozen framed photographs on the canopy above the bar. They were all of groups of grinning men holding big fish. Underneath each was a caption giving the names. Robert M. Ross appeared in four of them. Hallett must have seen them a million times before but he leaned forward and craned his neck back awkwardly to confirm their existence.

'That's him. Guy with the woolly hat. The best likeness is the end photograph there with General Aitchison and the twenty-six pounder.'

Fyfe went up on his tiptoes and looked more closely. His mind started ticking over, uncovering a memory that had been neatly filed away. It wasn't hard to find. The twinge of regret he had felt on hearing the case was solved vanished. He tried not to look too smug as he lifted the pint glass of lager and drank half of it straight away. Hallett was twitching behind the bar, just about managing to hide the shock he must have felt at the supposed discovery of a murderer among his workers.

'Nice dogs,' Hallett said. 'Do they go everywhere with you?'

'I wanted bloodhounds but these were all they had in the shop. This guy Ross? He a local?'

'He's been working here on the estate for about six or seven years now. I don't know where he came from originally. Edinburgh, I think. He never stops talking but, come to think about it, he wasn't keen on talking about himself a lot.'

'And he's the murderer, is he?'

'Damned out of his own mouth.'

'Tell me. What does the initial M in his name stand for?'

Hallett blew out his cheeks and sniggered. 'It's supposed to be a secret. He's really embarrassed about it. Swore me to secrecy because it so embarrassed him.'

'Go on then, embarrass him.'

'He tells the nobs it's for Malcolm but that's not the truth.'

'What is then?'

'Marion,' Hallett confided with an explosive snort of derision. 'I know it's a lassie's name but his father was a John Wayne fanatic. John Wayne's real name was Marion and Bob was landed with it.'

'Nasty trick to play on a boy,' Fyfe said. 'Can my dogs have a packet of crisps? Cheese and onion flavour is their favourite.'

'Certainly,' Hallett said. He poured crisps into a clean ashtray. 'There's your boss now.'

Fyfe got a glimpse of her in the mirror, all long legs and wide shoulders rippling over the bottles. He turned as she approached and saw that she was even more attractive than he had imagined. Her hand was held out in greeting and her eyes were shining triumphantly. He too would confess anything to those lovely baby blues. Her pleasure in having supposedly wrapped up the case was obvious. The smile on her face was designed to show Fyfe that he wasn't required after all. She thought she was in control and she was loving it.

'DCI Fyfe, I presume,' she said. 'Your reputation precedes you.'

'Nothing bad I hope.'

'On the contrary, but it looks as if you've had a wasted journey this time.'

He took her hand, squeezed it in sympathy and wondered briefly if it would be kinder to keep the truth from her and let her find out in due course. Her hand withdrew and he half-expected her to stick out her tongue.

He shouldn't delay, Fyfe decided sadly. Sometimes you had to be cruel to be kind. Better for her to find out now. The connections were made, the odds were shortened to almost negligible proportions. It was a small world, a smaller country. How many Robert Marion Rosses could there be hanging around the scenes of murders?

It was a shame but he was not going to be popular in the baby-blue eyes of Moya McBain. She was not after all going to instantly tumble into bed with him for some rest and recreation after a hard day's investigating. She was probably going to hate him. It was not a good start to their relationship. But what could he do?

'Nice to meet you, DI McBain,' he said.

'Likewise.'

He took her by the arm and attempted to lead her towards the door. He could feel the resentment in the tightening of her muscles, the digging in of her heels. This was her moment. She was calling the shots. It was her inquiry. She would determine whether she moved or not. He did his best not to sound too patronizing.

'Sorry about this, darling,' he said softly so no one else in the bar could hear. 'I don't mean to interfere but Robert Ross isn't your murderer.'

'What do you mean?'

'Trust me. You've got the wrong man.'

# 20

*Thursday 16.15*

It had sounded so convincing to Moya. Robert Ross had told of clandestine meetings by moonlight with his secret lover, Marianne. She was the daughter of one of the rich estate owners at Torridon. He didn't know which one. He didn't know her second name. All he knew was that there had been a potent sexual chemistry between them and they had conducted their furtive affair against moss-covered trees or beds of fragrant, fallen pine needles.

It was hopeless, of course, a Lady Chatterley-style relationship doomed to fail from the first kiss. When Marianne tried to break it off last night, Ross's only answer was an inarticulate violence that ended in her death.

Moya empathized with the broken man as he bowed his head and wept, explaining between heavy sobs how he had lashed out with his keeper's crook. A single blow had felled her, killed her. There was no heart beat for his searching fingers to find. No reaction when he grabbed her by the neck and tried to shake her awake. No retreat from his terrible act. No life in the body he had loved so intensely.

Ross had looked up at Moya then and she had to bite the inside of her lip to stop her own tears. Why did love have to be so cruel and why was she such a sucker for a hard-luck story, she was thinking.

He was not thinking clearly, Ross explained. He needed to perform some form of burial ceremony but Marianne was too beautiful to be buried in the ground at the mercy of worms and wild animals. So he rowed out to Parliament Rock and laid her on the platform there, a sacrifice for the gods. He knew she would soon be discovered. He wanted it to happen. He told how he knelt beside Marianne and recited a prayer as the dark waters of the loch moved restlessly around him and the cold of the night sucked the last of the warmth from her lifeless form.

It had all sounded so convincing, so utterly convincing. She had believed every word of it. The name wasn't right, but there would be an explanation for that, she was sure. A pet name. Lovers' name. She had visualized the crime of passion and seen tangible evidence of his emotional torment in the cuts the fishing-hooks had ripped in Ross's hands as he explained. It brought tears to her eyes.

She appreciated the romance, abhorred the violence. She patted the murderer on the back and told him she understood. She had wanted to question him more. Find out about the note stuffed into the victim's hand. The corroboration that made the story even more believable. Laura and Bobby, the tragic lovers. But David Fyfe had arrived and she had gone out to face the high-flying city cop sent to watch over her, and she had been confident she could rub the newcomer's nose in her instant success. The case was all wrapped up. She relished the opportunity to tell him she didn't need his help after all.

She told him. Politely, naturally, but she told him. And he had called her darling and abruptly kicked the feet from under her by telling her she was wrong.

Ross was a pathological liar apparently. Everything he had said had been lies, pure fantasy, pure invention. Fyfe knew it before he even heard him speak. Ross, it turned out, had used to make an unendearing habit out of wasting police time. He made up a story, picking details out of newspaper reports, and confessed to any murder that was available. Fyfe had had dealings with him ten years before in Edinburgh.

'He convinced me totally then,' Fyfe explained, and she knew he was just saying it to make her feel better. 'I bought everything he told me at first. Never for a moment suspected it was made up. He's a brilliant story-teller, relies on the suspension of disbelief factor. He likes looking you in the eye and seeing that you believe him. That's how he gets his kicks.'

Moya didn't know what to think, except that Fyfe was a patronizing bastard. She was embarrassed and angry. The niggling inconsistencies in Ross's tale now seemed glaringly obvious. She would have checked, of course. Bobby was a common enough name. Marianne was simply the wrong name. She would have found out it was all lies in the fullness of time. But she had been caught with her credibility round her ankles and she was ashamed of her own gullibility and foolishness.

Now she followed Fyfe into the hotel office where Ross was seated on a chair at the table. He was rolling a cigarette between stiff fingers covered in sticking plasters. He was wearing the fly-flecked woollen hat. Charlie Simpson was standing over him, smoking one of his roll-ups. Simpson too had said to her that the story had sounded a bit far-fetched but she hadn't been willing to listen.

Ross turned and looked blankly at Fyfe. Moya could see him thinking, frowning as he searched his memory to put a name to the new face. She saw realization dawn and the slight slump in his shoulders followed by the downcast eyes. He licked the Rizla paper and didn't look up.

Fyfe positioned himself on the edge of the desk so close to Ross his knee would have hit him on the jaw if he had moved it upwards. Simpson looked across to Moya, silently seeking an introduction.

'This is Detective Chief Inspector David Fyfe,' she said mechanically. 'He's come to keep us right on the investigation of murder cases.'

Fyfe pouted a little, and Moya wished she could act more professionally. It wasn't Fyfe's fault that she had screwed up, but it *was* his fault he had been sent to watch over her. The thought of her boss Ryder back at headquarters hearing about her naivety was making her break out in a cold sweat. Fyfe had said Ryder was an old friend. The bastards would be sniggering together behind her back.

Maybe she should be nicer to Fyfe, persuade him to gloss over her early failings. In the late-afternoon light from the French windows overlooking one corner of the ornamental garden he even seemed to convey a rough boyish charm. Those dogs of his were lovely animals. He couldn't be all bad if his dogs liked him, bastard that he was. Animals had a sixth sense about people.

'How you doing, Bobby old pal. Remember me?'

Ross raised his head slowly and reluctantly. 'No,' he said finally.

'I remember you. Robert Marion Ross. How could I forget a name like that?'

Ross did not react.

'Great story you came up with for me, Bob. The one about the old man in his flat down the docks. How many years ago was that now? I still have a hard time believing it's not true sometimes.'

Ross lit his roll-up. The constant movement of the adam's apple in his throat betrayed his nervousness. He sucked on the cigarette and chewed on a plaster on his finger. He looked shifty and untrustworthy. Moya could not believe how she had been so easily taken in by him.

'Remember yet?' Fyfe asked. 'The old guy Moloney? Supposed to be an IRA informer set up in a safe house by the Gardai for his protection? You? You were a hit man hired to get him. And according to you, you did. Knifed him to death because the gun the IRA promised you got lost in the post.'

Ross shifted uncomfortably on his chair. Simpson's face above him was a picture as he began to realize what was going on. A smile spread like the sun coming up. He looked directly at Moya. She looked down at the floor.

'Oh yes, it was a great story. Certainly had me going. For a whole day I was convinced. Then our colleagues in Dublin set the alarm bells ringing. No Moloney on their files. And you got the colour of the old man's shirt wrong. Didn't even know the number of his flat, or how many rooms, or what floor it was on. And the one big flaw I should have realized all along. Why should a professional assassin walk into the police station and give himself up. You remember your answer to that, Bob? Do you?'

Ross kept his head down. No reaction except another quick puff at his cigarette. Simpson was grinning from ear to ear. The tips of Moya's ears were burning. She bit her lip and avoided eye contact.

'You said you'd undergone a Born Again experience and had been converted to Christianity. There on the threshold of the murder scene, the bloody knife in your hand, you said you had found God. And so you had to confess your guilt and suffer the punishment.'

Fyfe sighed theatrically. He cocked his head to one side and gestured over to Moya as if to say 'you would never have believed a cock and bull story like that'. That he could have been so stupid did make her feel a little better, just a little. Behind her McIsaac coughed. She didn't turn round but she just knew he would be grinning as well. His time record for solving local murders looked safe again.

'Remember Bob? It's hard to credit that a man of my cynical nature could believe all that crap. But you're a brilliant liar. You're so fucking good you should have been a politician. And it looks like old habits die hard. You've been doing it again, haven't you Bob, with this tale of the lady in the loch? Back then I wanted the fiscal to lock you up for wasting police time. The fiscal declined to waste the court's time. I wasn't happy with that. I wanted you to learn your lesson. So what happened, Bob? Do you remember now?'

Ross stubbed out the cigarette and looked up for the first time since Fyfe had started speaking. His lip curled into a sneer. 'You kicked the shit out of me, Mr Fyfe.'

Fyfe smiled down benignly. 'Now is that the truth, Bobby, or is that just another one of your fantasies?'

Moya didn't have time to make a judgement. As the sentence finished Ross stood up, picked up the chair in one flowing movement and brought it crashing down on Fyfe's head. Fyfe went back over the side of the desk and landed heavily on the floor. Simpson made a grab at Ross and yelped when he got the chair over the knuckles. Ross threw it down and ran for the French windows, shouldering them open. The windows flapped back into a closed position and clicked shut. A delayed-shock effect made the glass turn opaque, shatter and begin to fall out in seeming slow motion. Rooted to the spot with shards of glass bouncing round her feet, Moya stood with her mouth hanging open watching Ross sprinting away.

# 21

Three guests out front tonight, and one waiting his turn in the back shop. Mr Beaumont. An elderly man. Heart failure while washing his car. Slight grazing on the left cheek where he had fallen, simply fixed with the application of a little smear of foundation cream.

In the rooms behind the main funeral parlour, Douglas Lambert watched as his young apprentice Robbie did the necessary and went on to trim the man's copious nostril hair without being told. It was hard to find youngsters willing to train as morticians. They usually ran a mile from the idea of handling dead bodies. Robbie was different. He was keen. He read *The Embalmer* from cover to cover and after six months in the public side of the job was shaping up nicely in his first week with the bodies behind the scenes.

'What is death but the natural consequence of living?' Robbie had said at the interview, showing a maturity well beyond his acne-plagued youth.

Lambert had been taken with that carefully rehearsed phrase. It summed up his own philosophy fairly accurately. A little humility went a long way in the undertaking trade, and attention to detail in advance preparation went that little bit further. Billy got the job despite his ear-ring and curious shaven-sides haircut. Lambert kept him working in the backshop out of sight of the relatives after a few complaints.

'Is that you finished then, young Robbie?'

'I think so, Mr Lambert.'

'Are you sure?'

Robbie held his chin and looked down on the mortal remains of Mr Beaumont. There had been a post-mortem. His internal organs had been removed, examined and then stuffed back, wrapped in newspaper. The chest cavity had been closed and clumsily stapled. All that didn't matter because he was now wearing his best shirt, tie and suit. His hands and face were the only parts visible. Robbie had cut his nails and painted out the nicotine stains on his fingers. He had combed his hair back and tidied his bushy eyebrows. The foundation cream hiding the graze could not be distinguished from real skin. Mr Beaumont looked fine, yet there was something wrong. Robbie stared and frowned.

'What haven't I done right, Mr Lambert?' he asked.

'His face. Look at his face.'

Robbie looked, put his head right down until he was almost nose to nose with the corpse. Then he straightened up and shook his head.

'What does he look like?' Lambert prompted.

Robbie frowned more deeply. He shook his head again.

'His expression. Look at his expression.'

Robbie looked. He narrowed his eyes, fiddled with his ear-ring, and looked very carefully. 'He looks kind of frightened or something.'

'Exactly. They're often like that, Robbie. It's the few seconds of remaining consciousness when they realize they're going to die and there's nothing anybody can do about it. You'd be frightened, wouldn't you?'

'I reckon.'

'It's usually sudden-death males who come in with fright frozen on. If they die ill in bed it's usually a look of sadness. Don't ask me why but females are much more likely to die smiling.'

'So what do we do?'

'Well, Mr Beaumont here is to occupy our rest room over the weekend until his funeral on Monday. It's to be an open coffin and we don't want his grieving relatives staring down on somebody who looks as if he has seen a ghost, do we?'

'No.'

'So what do we do about it, Robbie?'

Robbie grinned. 'We put a smile on his face.'

'You're a fast learner. But maybe not a full-blown smile. A

hint of one is better. I prefer the vaguely amused expression. You'll find that relatives are greatly comforted by it. Takes the edge off a solemn occasion.'

'But how do we do it?' Robbie asked eagerly.

'Like this.'

Lambert flexed his fingers and placed them on either side of the corpse's skull with the thumbs positioned below the cheek bones. He began to massage in small circular motions, feeling the stiffness of the flesh and the muscles below gradually give way under the steady pressure. He worked his way down over the cold surface until he reached the corners of the mouth. After a few minutes he stood back to admire his handiwork. Mr Beaumont's expression had changed. The look of fear had gone. Subtle contentment had settled on him.

'How does he look now?' Lambert asked.

'Much happier,' Robbie confirmed.

'Doesn't he? He's sleeping pretty now.'


## 22


*Thursday, 16.29*

Moya ran for the shattered windows but McIsaac and Simpson went past her and barged through first. She turned back to see if Fyfe was all right. He was lying on his back with his legs up on the desk. There was a cut oozing blood beside his left eye. As she crouched down beside him, wishing her skirt was not so short, she saw the swelling was already closing the eye in an obscene pantomime wink.

'Did you really kick the shit out of him?' she asked.

Fyfe leaned on her arm as he climbed awkwardly to his feet. 'Catch the bastard and I'll show you a repeat performance.'

Moya held on to his arm as they went outside. Ross had already managed to reach the jetty and untie a boat. He pushed away from the side and floated out, standing in the stern priming the motor before trying to start it. A panting Charlie

Simpson was next to board one of the boats, then a breathless Donald McIsaac, stepping inelegantly over the gap and falling into the bottom. A pair of navy divers came running after them, and another pair. One of the divers went straight into the water and began swimming towards Ross just as his outboard spluttered into life, churning the black water white and kicking the boat away from the shore.

Fyfe sat on the bench on the terrace of the ornamental gardens and let Moya hold a tissue against his bleeding eye. The swelling had closed it completely. He looked on in restricted mono-vision as the boat chase developed in front of them.

Ross was motoring now. Simpson and McIsaac were in pursuit. So was one of the navy boats. The other was delayed by having to pick his colleague out of the loch. Other policemen were untying some of the other boats. The occupants of the bar had poured outside, rounding the side of the hotel still carrying their drinks. Some went down to the jetty to shout encouragement. It wasn't clear whom they were encouraging. Jill was lying on the ground at Fyfe's feet with her head on her paws. Number Five was running up and down the path barking furiously.

'Why are we bothering to go after him anyway?' Fyfe asked. 'He's a loony. No fiscal is going to prosecute him for making up his daft stories.'

'They might prosecute him for police assault,' Moya suggested.

Fyfe patted his injured eye carefully. He winced a little to show her just how painful it was and enjoyed the look of concern on her face. The pain would hopefully deflect attention from his stupidity and slowness in allowing Ross to hit him over the head with the chair.

'Good point,' he agreed. 'How could I forget? Let's hope they don't drown him before they bring him back.'

'Oh no!' Moya leapt up. 'Look at that!'

'What?' Fyfe demanded to know. 'What is it?'

Moya pointed to the convoy of three boats rounding the headland and beginning to curve towards the shore. Fyfe saw a tall, round-shouldered man kneeling in the front of the lead boat with one hand resting protectively on a horizontal black shape. It was the body bag containing the murder victim. Fifty yards away he saw Ross's boat, riding a white bow-wave at the head of its own less sedate procession. Ross was looking back over his shoulder, concentrating on his pursuers. He didn't realize he was on a collision course.

'Talk about the Keystone Cops,' Moya said.

Through his one good eye Fyfe watched her watching the loch. From his position she had a lovely profile framed against the blue-grey sky. A cute snub nose and generous bust. Jill had sat up on the bench beside her and Moya was stroking her head and rubbing an ear between her fingers. Number Five came galloping back and forced her head under the other hand for similar treatment. By pretending to look at the dogs he could admire Moya's legs. A woman who appreciated his dogs, Fyfe thought, was his kind of woman.

'He's going to ram them,' Moya almost shouted.

Fyfe stood up to witness the final coming together. Everybody was standing up in the boats shouting, except Ross. The crowd on the jetty added their voices to the hubbub. The outboard motors droned like competing bluebottles. Number Five went racing back down the path. Moya clutched Fyfe's arm instinctively.

'Oh my God,' she said. 'He's going to ram them! Look out, Dr Eames!'

The tall man, Dr Eames, abondoned his semaphore act and dived overboard rather gracefully. His companion at the rear copied him. The two boats collided a few seconds later. The sound of splintering wood carried across the water to match the confused scene on the surface. Ross was thrown into the loch. His boat vanished from sight almost immediately and he was left thrashing about. The other boat, with a big hole chewed out of one side, listed dramatically, tipping the black body bag over the side. It floated away as the other boats began circling to pick up survivors.

'Don't let it sink,' Moya said. She spoke softly at first, then more loudly, more urgently. 'Don't let it sink. Don't let it sink. Don't let the bloody thing sink. Look at that. The fools are going to let it sink.'

She tugged at Fyfe's sleeve anxiously, frustrated by her land-bound helplessness. She cupped her hands round her mouth and yelled: 'Don't let it sink.'

But nobody could hear her out on the loch. Ross and the other two men were hauled on board as the black shape sank lower and lower in the water like a submarine slowly submerging. No one out on the water seemed to notice until it was too late. The body bag slipped from sight.

'For Christ's sake,' Moya stormed, stamping her foot. 'Keystone Cops did I say? Would you credit it? Have you ever seen anything like it?'

Fyfe shook his head in sympathy. He considered the idea of making some kind of joke about nobody being dead and at least she wouldn't drown, but decided against it. He didn't want to provoke her. Moya turned to face him. This time her hands were on her hips and a few strands had broken loose from her tightly scraped-back hair. Still seated, Jill shuffled round so that she was facing the same way. Number Five came bounding back up the path.

'I'm not doing too well, am I?' she said. 'Superintendent Ryder is going to love this. Not only did I lose my murderer but I go and lose my body as well.'

Moya laughed an instant before Fyfe did. They sat down on the bench again and she attended to his eye with the tissue. It might have been his imagination, but her touch seemed to be much gentler. They were bonding nicely after the false start.

'Don't worry,' he said. 'The divers will get your body back soon enough. What does it matter that she went for a swim before her post-mortem.'

'Fishermen would say it was the one that got away.'

'We'll get it back.'

They were interrupted by fat Joe Hallett. He stood at the back of the bench staring curiously down on Fyfe's injured eye. His presence made Moya become less flippant. She visibly stiffened and began dabbing at Fyfe's eye more firmly. Fyfe grunted, but exchanged a private smile with Moya that set them apart in their own little conspiracy against everyone else. On the loch the boats were returning to the jetty. Everybody was shouting at each other.

'Phone call,' Hallett said. 'They have an identity for our lady in white.'

'Who is she then?' Fyfe asked. 'The little mermaid?'

The joke fell flat. Moya stood up and headed inside to take the call. Jill and Number Five followed her. Fyfe walked behind at a distance, poking at the tender puffy skin round his injured eye.

'Traitors,' he said softly after the dogs so that nobody would hear. 'A right pair of bitches. All three of you.'

## 23

*Thursday, 17.18*

The lady in the loch was Laura Lambert. Resident of Edinburgh. Aged twenty-nine. Married. No children. Known to police records because of two convictions for possession of cannabis. Known to the rest of the world as a minor celebrity and fortune-teller. Her occupation was given as journalist and clairvoyant. A blurred mug shot was transmitted to the hotel by fax. In it she glowered furiously at the camera. Her hair was tied back. There was what appeared to be a bruise above her left eye but it might have been a smudge created in transmission. Fyfe brushed his own bruise in sympathy.

He had never heard of Laura Lambert but Moya remembered some kind of astrological game show that had graced the limbo of afternoon television a few years back. *Star Charts* it had been called and Laura Lambert had been the hostess; white teeth, plenty of leg, deep cleavage and embarrassing patter. She was sacked from the television after the second drugs case, a scandal that had briefly caught the interest of the tabloid papers before she had faded into spiritual obscurity. Until found semi-naked on a rock in the middle of Loch Maree with her head bashed in.

'I wonder if she saw it coming?' Fyfe asked.

'No more than any of us will when its our turn,' Moya said

enigmatically. 'I was into spiritualism once you know, after my mother died. It didn't last.'

'What does?' Fyfe said, handing the fax picture to McIsaac. 'Have you seen her around here before now, Donald?'

McIsaac studied the likeness on the piece of paper. He scratched his beard and shook his head. 'Holiday homes, holiday people. They come and go in their big cars. We never see them.'

'The husband's name is Wright, Simon Wright,' Moya said. 'Mean anything?'

'That name's more familiar,' McIsaac said doubtfully. 'Let me have a look at the council tax register I brought over. I'm sure there's a Wright in there somewhere.'

They waited while McIsaac went through the list on the bundle of continuous computer paper. It was in geographical not alphabetical order so it was a long job. Simon Wright was the next of kin. The address given was an up-market leafy part of Edinburgh. The machinery was already in progress to have him informed and questioned. Ryder was handling it from Inverness. He had also booked half a dozen hotel rooms for the troops in the front line.

'I was just going to do that,' Moya said.

'Phone him up and tell him you approve,' Fyfe told her.

'Why should I bother?'

'It's your case. Keep a grip on it. Let him know who's controlling it. It won't make any difference now but it will make him think twice before he does anything else off his own bat.'

She hesitated and then she did it, speaking over the phone slowly and clearly like somebody determined to get the words right when making an after-dinner speech. She kept up eye contact with Fyfe while she spoke. He would have winked at her but one eye was closed and the swelling had stretched the skin around the other too much.

'The body bag sank after the boat accident but we should be able to retrieve it soon,' she was saying. 'The guy who made the false confession is on the way to you now. Quite convincing he was but I soon saw through his story. He hit your friend Chief Inspector Fyfe over the head with a chair. Assault and resisting arrest should be the charge.'

69

Fyfe smiled encouragement and examined his injured eye in the window reflection. It was getting dark outside. The moon was hidden behind clouds, lightening the sky but making the darkness more intense at ground level. Ross was on his way back south, handcuffed in the back of a patrol car. The boats with the divers had formed a circle out on the loch. A couple of big spotlights run off car batteries had been rigged up and every winged insect from miles around was flocking to the phantom feast.

'Yes. He's here,' Moya was saying on the phone. 'No. No permanent damage as far as we can tell. Not a very warm welcome to our jurisdiction though, is it? We'll have to make it up to him somehow.'

Hallett knocked on the door. He was still shaking his head in bemusement over his misjudgement of the character of Robert Ross, good-natured ghillie turned raving madman. He said that Dr Eames and the others who had gone over the side into the water were showering and changing into clothes that didn't quite fit them. Oh, and the first newspaper reporters had arrived on the scene.

'Tell them we'll make a statement soon,' Fyfe said.

'Is that wise?' Moya asked.

'Get them on your side. They're going to write the story whatever we do so we have to make sure we get our slant on it.'

Moya looked out at the circle of lights on the water. It would be visible from the picture window in the bar too, impossible to ignore. She could see one guy with a bulky camera bag down by the jetty already. The aftermath of the Keystone Cops water-chase. The headline writers would be sharpening their witticisms. Poor Moya, Fyfe thought, it wouldn't look too good for her in the morning.

'Feed them some drink, Joe. Run up the profits and keep them busy. We can get Charlie to stall them. No names until next of kin informed and that kind of stuff.'

Here it is,' McIsaac interrupted suddenly, his index finger stabbing down on an entry on the list. 'Wright, Simon Henry. Torridon Cottage, Swan Bay.'

'That must be him,' Moya said.

McIsaac nodded enthusiastically. 'It's less than a mile from Parliament Rock as the swan swims.'

'Promising, promising.'

It hadn't taken the divers long to find the sunken body bag, Fyfe watched them struggle to haul the awkward black shape aboard. The boat rocked alarmingly and a beam of light flashed over the water, illuminating trees on the shore and the back of the hotel. The beam lit up the interior of the office momentarily and passed on. It picked out the sundial on its pedestal, casting a false time-telling shadow for less than a second before it was gone.

'When can we go there?' Moya asked.

Fyfe turned away from the window. He touched his chin and felt the light growth of stubble there beginning to spoil the smoothness of his skin.

'No time like the present,' he said. 'We'll throw some scraps to the media wolves and then head off.'


# 24


*Thursday, 18.24*


The headlights of Fyfe's car swiped across the rows of tree trunks on both sides of the rough track. They crowded in, shoulder to shoulder, right up to the edge, concealing what was behind them in the forest. Overhead the heavy branches leaned against each other, closing off the sky, completing the tunnel effect. Fyfe had a strong fatalistic sense of *déjà vu*, of dead bodies waiting to be discovered at the end of darkened tunnels. Silently, he began to move his lips to the words of The Grand Old Duke of York.

The car lurched slowly through potholes and over sharp-edged rocks. Its lights swayed erratically, bouncing from side to side off the trees. Clouds of midges drifted through the beams like shoals of tiny fish. Number Five stood with her paws on the back of the passenger seat and her head jutting forward over McIsaac's shoulder. Moya sat in the back with her arm round the dog. Jill sat beside her.

'Spooky, isn't it?' Moya said.

They had kept the reporters happy by feeding them an approved version of the story so far. Moya took the lead, posed for her picture to be taken, generally had them eating out of the palm of her hand. She gave them the woman in white on Parliament Rock to exercise their imagination. Case definitely being treated as murder. Can't go into details but I'm sure you can speculate imaginatively since nothing is ruled out. The boat collision was an unfortunate accident. Nobody hurt. Nothing to worry about. Nobody asked about the sinking and recovery of the body bag and she didn't volunteer the information.

The reporters had more than enough information to begin composing their stories and phoning them over. A mysterious woman in white was found dead on a mist-shrouded Highland loch yesterday, Fyfe heard, listening in on one call being made from the public phone. He and Moya were able to sneak away unnoticed.

'There it is!' McIsaac said dramatically, jabbing his finger against the inside of the windscreen.

Two bright red eyes suddenly glared out of the grey blackness. Fyfe stood on the brakes unnecessarily hard. Number Five's paws slipped off the back of the seat and she wrapped herself around McIsaac's neck. She yelped in surprise and Jill growled in sympathy. Moya dragged the young dog back into the rear.

'That's it there,' McIsaac said with his head bowed and his arm half-raised to fend off anything else that might fall on him from behind. 'That's it. Torridon Cottage.'

Close up, the red eyes became the reflective tail lights of a Range Rover parked askew with its front tyre in a flower-bed. Beside it the whitewashed walls of a squat single-storey house appeared in the headlights.

They were out of the tunnel of trees in a u-shaped clearing giving access to the loch. The sky was a lighter shade of dirty grey but at ground level the blackness persisted like a mist.

To one side a flatter expanse of darkness must have been the loch.

'Do you know who the Range Rover belongs to?' Fyfe asked McIsaac.

'Never seen it before.'

'It's not Laura's then?'

'It might be, I suppose. They're common as muck around here.'

'We'll get the number checked.'

Fyfe got out of the car first, leaving the engine running and the lights trained on the wall. A window had curtains drawn inside it. Rose bushes cowered underneath the ledge. The dogs jumped down onto the gravel before anyone could stop them. McIsaac spoke across the roof of the car.

'Did you bring a torch?'

Fyfe cursed himself for forgetting such an obvious thing. An owl hooted derisively.

'I've got one,' Moya said. 'Where's the door?'

McIsaac led the way out of the circle of light. The torch's thin beam was a poor replacement but it picked out a crazy-paving path with moss growing in the joints leading to an old-fashioned porcelain sink overflowing with muddy rainwater beside the door. Jill and Number Five both started drinking noisily from it. On the door was a cast-iron knocker in the shape of a leaping fish. Fyfe took hold of its tail and bashed it three times against the weathered wood panels. It made a hollow sound, like the beating of a drum, indicating emptiness. He waited only a few seconds before trying the handle. The door opened easily, hinges creaking hardly at all. The torch flitted over hanging coats, neatly stacked wellingtons, a sideboard with brass handles, closed doors standing sentry along the corridor.

'Where's the light switch?' Fyfe asked.

'No mains electricity here,' McIsaac replied. 'You'd have to start the diesel generator.'

'Where abouts is it?'

'Search me.'

'Okay then Moya, it's you and me and the torch. Stay close. Watch our backs Donald.'

Moya took him at his word. She stayed in close at his side,

her leg touching his, her hand holding his lower arm. They walked a few steps over the threshold. The dogs ran past them ignoring Fyfe's command to stay.

'You're not afraid of the dark, are you Moya?' he said.

'Of course not. Only of the things hiding in it.'

The first door on the right was not quite closed. Fyfe felt Moya's grip tighten as he gently kicked the door open with his foot. It moved a little way, then Jill and Number Five pushed in front and fought to get through the gap, throwing the door wide open.

The dogs started barking. The torchbeam showed slices of furniture, polished floorboards, a table stacked with magazines, ashes in a fireplace, pictures on the wall, and a figure rushing towards them across the room.

Moya screamed and dropped the torch. Fyfe stumbled backwards. The dogs barked furiously. Moya was outside the doorway but still clinging to him, her fingers digging deep into his arm. The room was blank darkness once more.

'What was it?' she demanded breathlessly.

'It's okay. It's okay. Shut up, will you, dogs.'

Fyfe was calm. The flicker of near-panic had stilled. He knew what the situation was. He had made sense of it through his one good eye. There was no need to be afraid of the dark, not now he knew what it was hiding.

'What was it?' Moya asked again.

'Nothing we can't handle.'

He picked up the torch. Moya reluctantly let go of him, staying where she was facing outwards with her back to the door jamb. The torchbeam sliced across the room; furniture, floorboards, fireplace, and a retreating figure this time going away from him. Number Five bumped into his leg but when he reached for her she was gone, still barking loudly.

Fyfe followed the wall round to the window. He pulled the curtains open and the room was flooded with bright light from the car parked outside. Jill and Number Five were standing side by side at the fireplace barking up at an arch-backed black cat on the mantlepiece. It was like a beautifully sculpted porcelain ornament. The light glinted on its green eyes and the icicle tips of its bone white teeth.

The hanged man swung across Fyfe's line of sight. Set in motion by the blundering entrance of the two dogs, he hung at the end of a rope in the centre of the room, knees slack, rotating more than swinging in a macabre slow motion tiptoe pirouette. The rope round the man's neck went up over an exposed ceiling beam and diagonally down to be anchored to a corner of the cast-iron fender surrounding the fireplace. The shadow the body threw was the largest among a seething fluidity of stark blacks and greys in the room. Glass-fronted pictures on the walls flickered like reels of silent movies.

'Come away,' Fyfe ordered sternly.

This time the dogs obeyed and stopped barking. The cat on the mantelpiece changed shape. It sat down, raised a paw to its mouth and began to lick it clean. It bumped a pendulum of half a dozen steel balls and started them swinging. The clicks counted the seconds. A low growl continued to rumble in Number Five's throat.

'Who is he?' Moya asked from where she stood in the doorway. McIsaac's bearded face peered over her shoulder.

'Our murderer?' Fyfe replied.

'That's two we've found in one day,' Moya said.

'Well, this one won't be confessing to anything. We'll have to work out the story for ourselves.'

The scenario that led to the hanged man unreeled of its own accord for Fyfe. Laura Lambert is killed in a fit of passion, laid out in tribute on Parliament Rock, suicide follows in a fit of remorse. So who was he? Husband? Lover? Candlestick-maker?

'The story looks promising from our point of view,' Fyfe said.

There was something wrong but he didn't yet know what it was. Moya came back into the room, McIsaac after her. Fyfe wanted to be optimistic but he always distrusted obvious explanations.

'Is this our murderer?' Moya asked.

'Could be.'

'A crime of passion followed by the suicide of the perpetrator. Neat isn't it?'

'All wrapped up for us.'

They exchanged doubtful looks. She sensed there was some-

75

thing wrong too, Fyfe realized. You're learning, he thought but didn't say anything because he didn't want to be patronizing. But there was definitely something not quite right.

The dead man was on tiptoe at the end of his rope, his shoes just scraping the floorboards and no more, knees hardly bent. McIsaac looked at his watch ostentatiously, catching their attention.

'Well, well, well,' he said. 'It looks like you might be beating my record after all.'

# 25

*Thursday, 19.14*

The wallet of documents Fyfe found in the glove compartment of the Range Rover suggested the hanged man was Ron Gilchrist. The name checked out as the registered owner and it was the same one on the credit cards in the hanged man's jacket pocket. No criminal record. Unless the vehicle was stolen, the police back in Edinburgh would soon be out breaking more bad news to grieving families.

Moya started organizing the scene of crime procedures and delegated to a sergeant as soon as the troops arrived, blocking the narrow track with their convoy of cars. The white-walled cottage was centre stage, illuminated by half a dozen pairs of headlights drawn up in a ragged semi-circle. A couple of navy men came out of curiosity, still wearing their wet suits, and stood at the fence. A couple of reporters too.

Dr Eames, dressed in borrowed clothes after his soaking, turned up in his little sports car and telescoped himself up from its low-slung chassis. As he approached the front door somebody discovered the generator had run out of fuel, poured in a handy can of diesel and flicked the switch. Bob Dylan was suddenly roaring out from the cottage:

'*I'm knock, knock, knocking on Heaven's door . . .*'

Everyone, inside and out, froze as if they were players in a game of musical statues. Then Charlie Simpson killed the music at source and everyone was able to move again. The invisible owl hooted its increasing annoyance at the disturbance in its domain.

Fyfe went down to the edge of the loch to use his mobile phone. Jill and Number Five went with him, the younger dog roamed around excitedly until she disturbed a big swan that hissed, opened its wings wide, extended its neck and made a clumsy warning charge. To Fyfe it was a white flicker against the dark background. Number Five came scampering back to hide behind his legs. That's why it's called Swan Bay, he thought, slapping at the voracious midges that swarmed around him.

He was standing over the rowing-boat that was probably used to ferry Laura's body out to Parliament Rock. It moved in slow rhythmic motion, almost imperceptibly, as if it was breathing. Somewhere out on the loch tiny waves were being created and running into the shore. Maybe it was the remains of all the activities of the day: the loch settling down again after all the fuss and bother. Eventually it would lie perfectly still, if nobody and nothing ever touched it again. Fyfe looked out over the black water and knew that perfect stillness was impossible to achieve.

He contacted Sally first to tell her he wouldn't be back that night. It took only the briefest of explanations to satisfy her. Then he phoned his own detective sergeant Bill Matthewson in Edinburgh and was passed round the building until he was found. Matthewson was a country boy from the north-west. He said he remembered McIsaac as the local bobby who had put him through his cycling proficiency test at primary school. A much more detailed explanation of events was needed to put him in the picture.

'I want you to find out who has got the job of breaking the bad news to this Simon Wright character and tag along with them,' Fyfe said.

'I won't ask why.'

'You know the way my mind works.'

77

'Only occasionally.'

'This is one of those occasions. Look him up and down. Let me know what you make of him.'

'Okay. Give my regards to Isotonic.'

'Who?'

'McIsaac. Isotonic was the nickname the kids gave him.'

'What does it mean?'

'I haven't the faintest idea.'

Number Five was getting restless and beginning to feel brave again. She went sniffing into the scrubby undergrowth between the trees and the loch. The flapping wings and loud hiss of an angry swan sent her scuttling back to safety. Fyfe killed a palm's-width of midges and led the two dogs back to the white-walled cottage in front of the battery of vehicle lights. He put them into the back of the Volvo. They went willingly but began to whine when they realized Fyfe wasn't going to follow them. Instead he called over McIsaac and told him to take the car up to the road-end to prevent any more reporters coming down. Fyfe mentioned Matthewson and McIsaac said he remembered the name. They laughed together about the Isotonic nickname. 'Something to do with athletes and muscle energy,' he explained from the driving seat. 'I looked it up in a dictionary once. I take it as a compliment.'

Fyfe stood by the Range Rover and watched the Volvo be absorbed by the darkness and the trees. There was a bundle of paper stapled together on the rear seat that no one had paid any attention to. He opened the door and took it out, noticing there were a few other similar bundles on the floor. Moya emerged from the front door of the cottage, shading her eyes from the blaze of lights. She had the right idea to keep the midges off, a piece of netting covering her face and held on by a baseball cap, but Fyfe hardly noticed because his attention had been seized by the paper bundle which turned out to be the proof copy of a magazine. It was not the title, *Ethereal*, which he had never heard of before. Nor was it the arresting cover image of a disembodied pair of eyes floating among fluffy clouds. It would be even more arresting in colour. The magazine seemed to be an airy-fairy New Age publication, relatively thin but obviously expensively produced in its final form, full of adverts for books on Tarot card readings, mystical pendants, and how to cook insects. It was Laura Lambert's name on the inside page, jumping out at him over the disproportionately big eyes of a stylized pen-and-ink drawing of the head and shoulders of the dead woman. There was absolutely no resemblance to the severe mug shot. In the drawing her mouth was an imitation of a Mona Lisa smile, her hair was a furiously swirling storm of twisted black lines. Her shoulders hovered in the white space below the headline: LEARN THE FUTURE WITH LAURA, PRINCESS OF PROPHECY.

Fyfe slapped at midges and started to read her column, trying to imagine the sound of Laura's voice. It would have been deep and husky almost certainly. Moya approached and she was about to speak when he raised a hand to stop her. He showed her the magazine and the page with the Laura Lambert column on it like a magician demonstrating he had nothing hidden in any of his equipment.

'Listen to this,' he said. 'And then tell me if it is spooky or what?'

He tilted the page a little to catch the strange light thrown upwards from the assembly of halogen beams and began reading aloud.

*'I know I must die and I know why. I have a vision of myself falling to the ground, toppling slowly like a heavy statue from its pedestal. And as I fall my killer rises. The rope tightens round his throat and squeezes from him the life he had to take from me. We are as one. It was a fateful bargain that we should die together in this manner. Two lives from the chrysalis of this world born anew in the butterfly heaven of the next.'*

'Spooky. Definitely spooky,' Moya said from behind her facial netting, moving on to Fyfe's shoulder so she could read it for herself. 'She did see it coming from a long way off then.'

Fyfe slapped a midge on his cheek. He rolled the tiny gritty remains under his fingertips until there was nothing left to roll. He felt something tickle the swollen skin round his injured eye and brushed it more gently. He continued reading.

*'I bear no grudge. I deserve my fate. Although my vision does not allow me to know the pain I shall be subjected to I believe it will be swift and transient. For him, briefly my master on this earth, the pain*

*will be more prolonged. It will contort his face into that of a devil incarnate. It is right and satisfying that the male of the species should suffer in death as the female suffers in childbirth. Death and birth are so similar in many ways and, of course, they are the portals through which we all must pass to achieve our destinies. I am human therefore I am afraid. But I am immortal and therefore I am at peace.'*

Fyfe looked up needlessly to check he had Moya's attention. She was hanging on every word. Someone came close and she waved them away impatiently. Her whole body was tense. She was standing so close to him he could feel her warm breath against his face.

'Now it gets really creepy,' Fyfe said. 'Nostradamus has nothing on this lady.'

'Come on. Keep going.'

*'I remember a swing I had as a child. I remember the rush of air against my face as I sat on it and was pushed by my father. My killer now feels the same gentle rush of air against his dead skin. He swings at the end of a rope that ends his brief span. It is as it must be.*

*'I remember also as a child one early morning my father rowing me out over mist-shrouded water to an island in a loch. There he put me ashore and made a game of pretending to leave while I wept and stamped my feet in frustration.*

*'This time my body will be borne to the island, clad in diaphanous white, and will be laid out there respectfully. I shall not weep, nor stamp my feet in frustration. This time there will be no pretence when the boatman rows away into the mist. It is to be my final resting place until I am found by unaware souls. I crave the touch of my rocky pillow and the sensuous feel of the breeze over the water. Do not grieve for me. The truth must be revealed. It is as it must be and I am content. Death waits and I will be truly at peace when the guardian of my soul howls at the moon.'*

Silence. The unseen owl hooted. Fyfe couldn't make out any expression on Moya's face behind the netting mask. The small of his back was damp with sweat. The moon was momentarily exposed through the racing clouds and the wind-shifting tree-tops clawed at it, failing to get a grip.

'Suicide pact firmly back in the frame,' Fyfe said. 'She saw it coming all right. She wrote a travel brochure about it.'

Moya snatched the magazine from him and began to read the

column for herself. 'The laws of prophecy have just come back to me from my spiritual phase,' she said. 'One is that the most obvious interpretation is likely to be wrong. Recently confirmed by my friend Ross.'

'How many laws are there?'

'As many as you want. Another is the law of non-existent impossibility. If it can happen it will; if it can't, it might.'

'Well that leaves our options wide open,' Fyfe said. 'I still fancy the suicidal option though.'

'Of course prophecies can be self-fulfilling too.'

'Of course.'

They both became aware of Dr Eames standing a little way off from them. The collar of his borrowed shirt was far too big, his overcoat too small. His eyes were bloodshot and blinking furiously.

'I thought you'd like to know my preliminary findings,' he said.

'Go on then, Doc,' Moya replied.

'The rope from which he is hanging didn't kill him. There is a mark on his neck made by a much narrower ligature. Suicide seems unlikely if not physically impossible. I think you should mark this one up as murder number two. I'll know more after the post-mortem. Speak to you tomorrow.'

Eames went over and folded himself down into his little MG. It took several shimmies back and forward to get the car pointed in the right direction to exit. Its red tail-lights shone briefly like animal eyes among the black mass of the forest and then were gone.

Fyfe looked at Moya and killed a midge on his forehead. The slap made his injured eye throb painfully.

'As I was saying,' he said. 'Let's keep all our options open.'

# 26

Ron's dead. There was no painless way to break the news. They came to the door. They said they were sorry but Ron's dead. From wife to widow in a fraction of a second. Patricia Gilchrist examined her new self in the tall mirror. There was too much grey in her hair. She would have to dye it. Black was the proper colour of mourning.

The policewoman had stayed when the others left. She was a small, dumpy young girl with a surprising amount of hair bundled on the back of her head beneath her cap. She made sweet tea and Patricia couldn't understand where she had found the sugar because she was sure there was none in the house. Neither of them took sugar in their tea anyway. They sat and drank it by the light from the lamp with a picture on the shade of the coach and horses racing past an inn.

'I'll have to identify the body,' she told the mirror.

'I'm afraid so,' the young policewoman confirmed.

Murder they said. Someone had murdered Ron. She had got up from her armchair in the almost suffocatingly warm living-room. She had put down her glass of mulled wine and her romantic novel and uncurled her legs from beneath her. She had gone to answer the doorbell. Ron's dead, they told her. He's been murdered.

In the mirror behind her she could see the armchair where Ron would normally have been sitting. He had gone north on business, called away suddenly that afternoon. He had warned her he might have to stay overnight. Now he wasn't coming back. Opposite the empty chair she could see her own chair, also empty. The cushions still held the moulded shape of her body.

'Take a seat, Mrs Gilchrist.' The policewoman tried to nudge her towards the armchair. 'Why don't you sit down?'

'I answered all their questions, didn't I?' Patricia asked.

'Yes you did.'

'They'll want to ask me more.'

'Probably.'

Laura had not been mentioned. Not yet at least. But she had heard the news on the radio about the woman found dead at Loch Maree. The old fool had slavered and lusted after Laura. It had been so pathetically obvious, even if he had never actually done anything and she could safely ignore it. Now he had been found dead in her cottage in the Highlands. O God, what had he done. What an embarrassment this was going to be. How was she going to face people?

'I have to make some phone calls,' she said.

'Of course.'

'Private calls. I'd like to be alone.'

'Naturally. I'll be in the kitchen if you need me.'

Patricia picked up the phone. The number was so familiar she did not have to look at the dial as she punched it out. Three double rings then she hung up and dialled again immediately. It was answered on the first ring the second time.

'Ron's dead,' she said.

'I know,' said the voice at the other end of the line. 'Didn't I tell you everything would be all right?'

## 27

*Thursday, 21.33*

Janet Dunbar gathered up her clothes frantically and darted into the kitchen just before they entered the living-room. What the hell was Simon playing at inviting whoever-it-was into the house? She had tried to get him to ignore the doorbell. They were, after all, rolling in well-lubricated carnal abandon on the carpet when it began to ring. It was easy enough to shut out the sound at first. But it kept going, stridently and insistently, demanding a response. Finally, Simon couldn't stand it any longer. Anyone could see the lights in the house and the cars in the drive, he reasoned. They weren't going to go away until somebody answered the door.

He got up, pulled on his trousers and his sweat shirt and went bare-footed to see who it was. She was left lying on her back staring up at the ceiling in silent frustration.

Janet couldn't believe it when she heard him bringing them in. He talked loudly as they got closer. He was banging the doors, moving slowly, sending a warning that she should make herself scarce. So she scooped up her clothes and headed for the kitchen where the coldness of the floor made her hop from foot to foot. She got dressed hurriedly, standing by the slightly open door to be able to listen to what was going on in the lounge. She wondered if she should make an entrance now that she was decent and brazen it out. The dinner-table was laid for two after all. The dessert plates were still in place, the candles guttering low. It would be fairly obvious he wasn't alone.

But she was a married woman and her affair with Simon hadn't been going long enough for her to be sure of her ground. A mere four weeks was their track record, and most of that had been taken up with the sharing of physical needs rather than the sharing of confidences. She didn't know him well enough to judge how he would react if she walked in on some kind of delicate situation. And it certainly must be delicate for him to interrupt a love-making session in full flow.

She didn't know his friends, didn't know his enemies. All she knew was that he was quite wealthy, quite good-looking and separated from his wife. She screwed her eyes tightly shut for several seconds and opened them again. She kicked at the door, making sure she missed it. Good God woman, she raged at herself. What are you doing here?

There was more than one visitor. A woman was talking. Somebody else was moving round the room, casting a shadow over the edge of the kitchen door. Janet flattened herself against the wall inside.

'We don't know the full facts yet, sir, but we wondered if you could help us in any way.'

'We have been separated for several months.' He hesitated,

looking round the room as if to ensure no one else was there. 'I haven't seen her for weeks now.'

'Did she have another partner?'

'Probably. Laura wasn't the sort of person who liked being on her own.'

'Can we ask if that contributed in any way to the break-up of your marriage, Mr Wright?'

'What do you mean?'

'Her relationship with another man?'

'No. There was no other man. Not that I was aware of. It was an irretrievable breakdown. I didn't understand her any longer. She didn't understand me so she went home to her father.'

'Was it an amicable separation?'

'Not really. There was lots of shouting and bitching.'

'Bad?'

'Not pleasant. But there was no violence if that's what you're getting at. I didn't kill her.'

Janet's curiosity had her almost putting her head round the corner but she resisted the temptation. It was making sense gradually. The visitors were police. Laura was dead. Laura, the estranged wife she had never met but whose perfume never seemed to fade. Her photograph was on the back of the bathroom door, the face riddled with holes from the set of darts that was kept there in the basket with the bars of sweet-smelling soap. Whenever Simon was in the bathroom she would hear the darts thumping into the wood. Janet was secretly self-conscious about her resemblance to Laura; not so dark, nose a different shape, but close enough. Simon never talked about her. Janet didn't like to mention it. What had Laura done to him?

The policewoman spoke. 'We'll be able to provide you with more information tomorrow, sir.'

Then the policeman. 'And we'll be asking you more questions as well. You're not intending going anywhere, are you?'

'No. I'll be here or at my office. Have you told her father yet?'

'We're just on our way there now,' said the woman's voice. 'Unless you want to contact him first.'

'No. It will be better coming from you. We never got on.'

They were going. The outside door banged. Janet risked

peeping round the kitchen door. The living-room was empty. One candle had burned itself out and a thin line of smoke was rising straight up to the ceiling. The other sustained only the tiniest of flames. Simon's socks were half concealed by the cushion under which she had hurriedly stuffed them. Simon himself came back into the room. A broad grin was on his face, but it was not a smiling grin, it was more a shocked sort of grin. He held his arms wide and cocked his head to one side.

'Marry me Janet,' he said.

'I beg your pardon.'

'Marry me Janet. I'm a free man now.'

He embraced her, squeezing her firmly against his body. When he stepped back his face had collapsed into an expression of pure grief and his eyes were brim-full of tears. Janet was frightened by the incongruity of his actions. Her whole body was cold despite the warmth in the room. She had to get away as quickly as she could.

'What do you mean?' she asked knowing exactly what he meant because of what she had overheard.

'I'm a free man. I'm no longer married.'

'How come?'

'That was the police. They came to tell me my wife has just been found dead. I'm a widower.'

Janet didn't know what to say. All she could think of was the heavy thud of the darts tearing into Laura's photograph. She took him in her arms so that she didn't have to look at him. He was sobbing now, a heavy weight on her shoulder. Good God woman, she told herself. Get the hell out of here quick.

'How did it happen?' she asked tentatively.

He shook his head. She felt his nose squashed against her collar bone. He said something but she couldn't make it out.

'Pardon,' she said.

He moved back to look at her. The strange grin was back. His cheeks were wet with tears, his eyes blurred with pain. 'Murder,' he said.

Janet swallowed the excess saliva that flooded into her mouth. The gulping sound seemed inordinately loud. He embraced her once more, resting his head on her shoulder. His steady sobbing made her body tremble as well. She patted the back of his neck.

'I'm sorry,' she said.

'Don't be sorry,' he replied, giving that disarming little smile of his. 'Be my alibi?'

# 28

*Thursday, 21.35*

After the police had told him about his daughter's death and gone away Douglas Lambert went downstairs from his flat to the funeral parlour. In the workroom at the back Mr Beaumont's corpse lay on the table covered by a single plastic sheet. His coffin, an oak top-of-the-range, satin-lined affair, had been delivered in the late afternoon but Robbie had gone by then so the transfer had been put off until the next morning. The coffin stood waiting on a pair of trestles.

The police asked questions about Laura and he had answered them as best he could. She had been back staying with him for about six or eight months since leaving her husband. He took them up to Laura's bedroom and watched them go through the drawers and wardrobes. He knew there was nothing to be found.

Did Simon know? Yes. Good. No, he hadn't known where she was. He hadn't seen her for a few days. Nothing unusual in that. She came and went. Yes, there was a man in her life, but it was a delicate subject. Name of Robert, he believed. Bob. But he had never met him, never asked about him. No idea of an address. Yes he knew about the cottage in the Highlands. He had stayed there himself, gone fishing. Ron Gilchrist? Yes. They had served short-term commissions in the Gordon Highlanders together. Of course Ron knew Laura. He was a family friend. Dead? Ron? In the cottage. How strange. He could think of no reason why Ron should be there. None at all. Had Ron's wife been told? Yes. Good. Poor Patricia. She would take it badly.

Lambert stripped back the sheet and Beaumont's gently smiling dead face shone waxily in the lamplight.

The grieving widow had called. She had changed her mind. Didn't want an open coffin any more. Didn't want to see her husband in that state. Could the coffin be sealed please. Sorry for any inconvenience.

Lambert placed his thumbs against Beaumont's cheek bones and slid his fingers round the sides of the skull. He began to massage, pulling at the corners of the mouth, pressing hard. The smile disappeared. A frown replaced it temporarily. Lambert eased the lips apart, exposing the teeth. He prised the eyes open, showing only the cloudy whites. As he massaged the face took on the form of a snarl and then a succession of different expressions like a kaleidoscope of moods that had come and gone during his life. Satisfied at last, Lambert lifted the stiff body in his arms and carried it over to the coffin.

Beaumont's dead eyes stared upwards. His mouth gaped in a frozen rictus of death, caught in a silent scream of abject terror.

'That's more like it,' Lambert said as he slammed the lid.

Upstairs again, he went into Laura's bedroom and thought about the last time he had seen her alive. The picture was vivid and detailed, the very pattern of the wallpaper with its flat forest of red and green flowers was intimidatingly familiar. Laura his little girl, turning before his eyes into a sullen, uncommunicative teenager, and then a beautiful woman. And as her body changed and matured so did her mind, from respectful admiration to spitting contempt and hatred. Dazzled by her good looks, few people seemed to realize just how much of a slut she had become before the end. A father couldn't stop loving his daughter but he could stop believing in her. He had long ago reached that stage. It was very sad.

Laura had been standing by the edge of the bed holding Bobby's head against her stomach underneath her T-shirt. It had been a private moment, a terrible moment. He knew then that they must have succeeded in their self-centred plan. Laura regarded him with undisguised scorn. Bobby sneered, blowing bubbles from tongue-wet lips. It was the last time he had seen Laura alive.

The phone rang three times and then stopped. He recognized

the code and knew who it was. Pat would need consoling. So did he. He snatched the phone up on the next ring. Everything would be all right.

# 29

Somewhere in the hotel a grandfather clock struck midnight. The chimes sounded crystal pure in the distance. Fyfe sat on the chair by the dressing-table with a glass of whisky in one hand and a damp cloth pressed to his eye in the other. Jill and Number Five were flat out beside the bed. Moya lay on her back on top of it with her legs crossed demurely at the ankle and an opened-out proof copy of *Ethereal* magazine covering her face.

'Is that the time?' she asked from under the pages.

'No,' Fyfe replied. 'It's five minutes slow at least. It's later than you think.'

'My daughter's hijacked my watch, you see.'

'That's what daughters do. What's your daughter's name?'

'Isabel.'

'Does she look like you?'

'A bit.'

'She must be lovely then.'

'Right that's it.' Moya lifted the magazine from her face and swung her legs off the bed in the same motion. 'Time for bed.'

'I thought you'd never ask,' Fyfe said.

'Your own bed. We've got work to do in the morning.'

Fyfe tossed the cloth into the wash-hand basin and sat back. He held up the whisky glass to indicate that he would go as soon as it was finished. She relented and reached for her own half-full glass of gin and tonic. She took off her ear-rings and shook them in her free hand like a pair of dice.

'I've got a daughter,' Fyfe said. 'Her name's Kate.'

'Does she look like you.'

'Not a bit.'

'Lucky girl.'

Moya laughed raucously and collapsed back on the bed. Jill looked up curiously, then put her head back down on her paws. Moya was slightly drunk. She hadn't eaten much of the food Fat Joe had scraped together when they got back from the cottage, leaving it to the recalled forensic team who would have to travel out from Inverness again in the morning. They ate with Charlie Simpson and Isotonic. She was too excited, too full of the personal experience of finding Gilchrist's body hanging on a rope in that darkened room, too concerned about analysing the various possibilities and assessing the odds.

Case conference over a couple of bottles of Hungarian Bull's Blood and heated up chicken kiev brought them back to earth. Forget the supernatural and the paranormal. The explanation for Laura Lambert's column describing her own death down to the last detail was obvious. The murder was predicted because the murderer, not Laura, wrote the script. Therefore, find out who had written the column and you had your murderer. Simple. Case closed.

Fyfe and Moya had agreed they should go to Edinburgh as soon as possible to follow up that line of inquiry. She would stay at the flat he and Sally owned in the New Town. The lawyers were still chasing the last tenants for rent arrears. Soon he intended to sell it and put the proceeds in yet another, much smaller, biscuit tin under his garden shed.

It was then Moya rather shamefacedly produced the evidence bag with the note in it. She had forgotten all about it in the flurry of activity caused by Robert Ross's bid for freedom and then the journey through the forest to find the hanged man. But here it was on the table alongside the half dozen rough copies of *Ethereal* magazine that had been found in the back of Gilchrist's Range Rover. It was another element. Another possibility, and a very useful one too. A comparison of writing would be critical in building a prosecution case against somebody.

'I can see how you were taken in by Bob Ross,' Fyfe said.

'The name fitted. It just all fell into place.'

'And straight out again. Never mind. This is either a deliberate false trail or a cry for help.'

'How do you work that out?'

'Well, the criminal psychologist who will no doubt be foisted upon us if this inquiry goes on past the weekend will say two things. One: the murderer is extremely clever and cunning and displays his intelligence by taunting those who are appointed to catch him. Or two: the murderer is driven by uncontrollable impulses but has enough self-awareness to realize the wrongness of his actions. He wants to be caught so he leaves a trail of clues so we can find him.'

'Which one is it then?' Simpson asked.

'Depends on the psychologist.'

'I would have said it depended on the murderer.'

McIsaac left, and Simpson went up to his room, slipping past the bunch of reporters who were still drinking in the other bar. Fyfe had escorted Moya up the creaking stairs. The dogs went too and invited themselves in. Fyfe tried to make them follow him but really used it as an excuse to hang around and chat for almost an hour. Now it was time to leave well alone. The mildest of flirtations was sufficient. After all, professional colleagues shouldn't go all the way on the first date.

'I'll let you have Number Five to keep you company,' Fyfe said as he poured the remainder of his whisky down his throat. 'Come on Jill. Come on girl.'

Jill got to her feet, stretched, and followed him to the door. Number Five cocked an eyelid to watch but made no attempt to follow.

'She likes you,' Fyfe said.

'It's mutual,' Moya replied from the bed.

# 30

*Friday, 01.20*

It seemed like the right thing to do. Douglas Lambert lay on his back in bed and Patricia Gilchrist slept in the crook of his arm. Her weight had long since slowed the circulation and cut off all feeling but he made no attempt to move the arm. He couldn't sleep himself. Instead he studied the ornate cornice in the unfamiliar bedroom, all the time thinking that it was indeed working out for the best just as he had promised. He had handed the organization of the next day's funerals to his down-the-line managers. In the morning Pat and he would go north together to identify the dead bodies of their loved ones.

He had bought a good bottle of wine and a box of chocolates and taken a taxi round to the row of terraced houses where Pat lived. There was a group of about half a dozen reporters in a pair of cars parked on the opposite side of the well-lit street. They watched the taxi as it cruised along the street with the driver peering out trying to make out the individual house numbers. Just as the driver reached it, Lambert ordered him to go on past. He got out round the corner and dialled Pat's number from a phone box. He used the three-ring code and she answered immediately on the second call. When he walked back along the street the reporters again watched him suspiciously. They began to get out of their cars when he knocked on the door. But Pat was waiting to open it immediately. They were only halfway across the road when he slammed it shut behind him.

Lambert and Pat had stood in the vestibule looking at each other, ignoring the sound of frustrated reporters hammering on the door and ringing the bell. After a few minutes they gave up and went away. Lambert held up the plastic bag containing the wine and chocolates. It was a confused peace offering. Now that they were face to face he didn't know what to say. It looked like he wanted to celebrate.

'Did you kill Ron?' Pat asked simply.

'No.'

'He didn't kill Laura. You know that.'

'Yes I know that.'

'The old fool lusted after her but he didn't have it in him to kill her. He didn't.'

'No.'

'What do you think happened then, Doug?'

He shook his head, pleading ignorance. 'It will all make sense eventually, I suppose.'

She embraced him tightly. The top of her head pressed against his chin, forcing his head back. She clung to him as they went into the house and hardly let go of him until they got into bed. There was no sex. He didn't try. They were just two old friends suffering from the pain of bereavement in need of mutual comfort.

Round the edge of the ceiling, the moulded pattern of the plaster cornice repeated itself every few feet. A raised line picked out in gold paint ran through it like a thread stitching the walls to the ceiling.

He had been sleeping with Pat, on and off, for the best part of twenty years but he had never before slept with her in this bed. It had been a long-running affair, yet totally discreet and secret. They each had a different life outside it and didn't want to jeopardize that. Their friends would have been shocked.

He couldn't put a date to his change of attitude when he started wanting Pat to be with him all the time instead of on irregular occasions. It was relatively recent and Pat was having none of it. The last time they had parted it had been after a blazing row. She was content to continue as normal. She wasn't going to leave Ron for him. She just wasn't. Ron might drool embarrassingly over young girls and take her for granted, but he was her husband and she had no intention of dumping him at this stage in her life. She didn't want things to change. She was too old and set in her ways. Damn it, she was too respectable. So was Lambert. Respectability was too important. They had kept their secret too long and too well. They were both too staid and respectable to suddenly reveal themselves as passionate lovers.

But now Ron was dead and in a manner that blew apart her cherished respectability. Things had changed whether Pat liked it or not. She was still in shock for the time being but she would come to realize it quickly enough.

'Are we celebrating?' she had asked as they drank the wine.

'We're mourning,' he had replied.

He had always been honest with Pat, never told her any significant lies. Three times she had asked him if he had killed Ron and three times he was able to deny it. Three times she held his stare for a long time in that way she had of making sure he was being absolutely genuine. Three times she was satisfied he was.

'He wasn't sleeping with Laura,' Pat had said.

'I know.'

'It was just silly flirting. I mean you knew about Laura, didn't you? She was back living with you, after all. You must have known.'

'I knew about him and Laura,' he agreed. 'Sometimes I think she made a big show of it just to annoy me.'

'So what do you think happened up there?'

'Maybe we'll never know. She was changing all the time. I didn't understand her any more. She was a mystery to me.'

'She did say the most awful things about you.'

'Yes.'

'I don't know how you put up with it.'

'She was my daughter.'

'Your cross to bear.'

'Exactly. Nobody else's.'

In the enclosed bedroom with the ceiling tightly stitched to the walls Lambert carefully eased his arm out from under Pat and began rubbing it to restore the circulation. Painful prickling spread along the length of the arm as he flexed his fingers and the blood and the feeling returned.

# 31

*Friday, 06.13*

The mist lay a few feet deep over the surface of Loch Maree like a rumpled white tablecloth. McIsaac expertly steered the boat in towards the makeshift tarpaulin tent that marked Parliament Rock. Fyfe sat in the middle of the boat with Jill at his feet. Number Five had been left back at the hotel, undisturbed in Moya's room, because she couldn't be trusted not to jump over the side and go chasing after the ducks.

Fyfe had snatched a few hours' sleep in his room, but seemed to have barely closed his eyes before McIsaac was knocking on the door ruining the dream that had just reached the stage where Moya was climbing into bed beside him. His first attempt at sleep had been disturbed after ten minutes when Matthewson had called around one, definitely fingering the husband Simon Wright as a prime suspect. Others had done the rounds of Laura's father, a sad-eyed undertaker, and Gilchrist's wife, a well-preserved lady of leisure with equally sad eyes. They had received pass marks while Matthewson had personally visited Wright and come away with a very bad impression.

'He acted shocked all right, but there was something about him,' Matthewson had said. 'Oily type. A lawyer. I wouldn't want my sister to marry him. I reckon quite a lot will crawl out from under his stone once we start questioning him properly.'

Fyfe agreed with him but couldn't help thinking back to one of the laws of prophecy Moya had told him about; the most obvious interpretation is likely to be the wrong one. He arranged for Wright to be brought in for questioning the next afternoon. Better for him to be taken in than for them to go to him. Show him who's in charge. Get him sweating a bit.

'Give my regards to Isotonic,' Matthewson had said.

The next person Fyfe saw was McIsaac, trimly turned out in uniform and silver beard, betraying no hint of the lack of sleep he too must be suffering. Fyfe crawled out of bed reluctantly to answer the knock, stumbling over Jill. McIsaac was standing to attention on the other side.

'Morning, Isotonic,' he said.

'Good morning yourself, sir. You slept well, I trust.'

'I did. Must be the Highland air. Your old biking pal sends his regards.'

Fyfe rubbed his chin. It was less than twenty-four hours since he had been shaved by Sergio in the barber's shop but it already felt coarse to the touch, though not enough to make it worth his while shaving. The swelling round his eye had settled down to a fairly extensive blue and purple smudge with the white of the half-shut eye a deep pink. Sitting on the toilet he again read Laura's column in the magazine and wondered at its exotic strangeness.

Fyfe didn't have a change of clothes so he sprayed himself with borrowed deodorant and put the same underwear and shirt and jacket back on. He knocked gently on Moya's door and was relieved when there was no answer. It gave him longer to think of a good opening line to begin their second day of acquaintance. He went downstairs and borrowed a Barbour from the coat-stand in the lobby and followed McIsaac out into the frosty atmosphere. Fyfe hadn't seen the rock where Laura's body was found and wanted to do so before heading south for Edinburgh.

'Best part of the day, don't you think sir?'

'I've seen worse.'

Dawn had broken as they pushed away from the jetty. The chuntering of the outboard motor shattered the early morning quiet and sent a couple of moorhens fleeing over the mirror-smooth water. The air above the transparent mist was icily clear. The pine trees on the islands were decorated with glistening droplets of water. The mountain ridge on the north shore and the rounded summit of Slioch were pinprick sharp against the lightening sky. The boat moved steadily across the loch. Neither man spoke much until the rock and the tent on top of it were very close. Fyfe jumped ashore and tied the mooring rope to one of the scaffolding poles. McIsaac clambered after him. Jill sat in the boat watching them.

There was very little to see on the rock. Inside the tent was a chalk outline of Laura's body, nothing else. There was no sense of hovering spirits, or supernatural entities, or doorways to different dimensions. He stared down at the patterns of lichen and tried to see something, anything. It was like looking for flame animals in the embers of a fire. Nothing.

What was written in the magazine? 'I am human therefore I am afraid. But I am immortal therefore I am at peace.'

Stirring stuff. Whoever murdered Laura had a poetic soul. And there was the handwritten note from Bobby asking for forgiveness. Only to be expected really. Every poet has a troubled conscience.

Fyfe came out of the tent and walked to the far end of the rock. He could see a pair of swans on the loch but not the cottage where the body of the hanged man had been found. It was masked by the trees that crowded right to the very edge of the water.

'Do you believe in reincarnation, Donald?' Fyfe asked, dipping the toe of his shoe into the crystal clear water.

'One life's enough for me,' McIsaac replied.

'Same here.'

# 32

*Friday, 07.40*

Moya opened her eyes and a tremor of fear stiffened her whole body. There was somebody in the bed behind her. She could feel the weight on the mattress dragging her in towards the centre. She could feel the solid contact and when she lay completely still she could feel the steady, rhythmic movement of a rib-cage pressed against her back.

What had she done? She should never have had that late-night drink after such a long and tiring day, but it seemed so churlish to refuse and they were making good progress on the case. It was important to keep the momentum going so they had camped in the bar with the reporters barred and Fat Joe in his dressing-gown and stripy pyjamas shuffling around in the background, still unsure whether the abrupt notoriety of his hotel would be good or bad for business in the long term. McIsaac was the first to go, driving away in a crunch of gravel. Then Charlie Simpson with an exaggerated yawn and stretch. And suddenly it was only her and Fyfe and they took a bottle and went up to her room. She didn't like to say no. Late night drinking conferences were part of the job, when thinking became lateral and ideas came thick and fast. She was one of the boys. She couldn't not agree to it.

And what had happened then? She couldn't remember. There was a vague picture of Fyfe standing over the bed looking down on her. She had eaten so little during the day. The drink must have gone straight to her head. What had she said? What had she done? What would he think of her?

He was moving. The weight at her back was shifting. She tensed so much her muscles hurt. Her nightdress was bunched awkwardly round her waist. By moving her fingers slightly she was able to make sure she was wearing knickers. A small mercy.

He was on top of the bedsheets. He must have fallen asleep there beside her. It was all perfectly innocent and she didn't know if she was glad or sad. Nothing had happened after all.

She closed her eyes. She could feel his hot breath against the top of her head. It smelled awful. And he was pressing hard on her shoulder and breathing strangely, panting almost. What the hell was he doing? Surely not now? Not in the morning. Something cold and wet touched her cheek. What did he think he was doing? A rough tongue scraped across her forehead.

She squealed and threw off the covers to jump out of bed. She turned back ready to hit out and shout abuse but was stopped by the sight of a black labrador sitting on the pillow with its pink tongue hanging out the side of its mouth.

'Number Five,' she said, realizing the fortunate truth. 'We must stop meeting like this.'

Only a few seconds had passed between Moya regaining consciousness and Number five licking her face. The idea that she might have slept with Fyfe had been no more than a fleeting thought. Now her mind was functioning properly and she was able to recall saying goodnight and going to bed alone before falling into an exhausted sleep immediately.

Moya picked up the magazine and slowly read Laura's column once more, trying to squeeze the last ounce of significance from every word. It was so obvious, of course, in the clear light of day. So much for the spiritual dimension. So much for the supernatural. It was a real flesh and blood crime, after all. What was it Fyfe had said? The murderer wanted to be caught. Hopefully they would be able to oblige.

She flicked back to the title-page of the magazine and reminded herself of the name of the editor, Edward Illingworth, and the office address in Edinburgh. He would be worth talking to. The publisher Ronald Gilchrist would be unable to assist their inquiries. She would get the house-to-house rolling up here, and a fingertip search of the forest within a half-mile radius of the cottage. She and Fyfe had agreed their time would be best spent heading south to see what Wright and Illingworth had to say for themselves.

Moya went over to the window and pushed back the curtains. The pale dawn light spilled through the dirty glass panes and poured round her. The horizon was stained red. Snow patches and black shadows gleamed in crevices near the summit of Slioch. Boats were clustered round the hotel jetty. Another boat was approaching it, trailing a long, curving v-shaped wake behind it. She recognized McIsaac at the stern and Fyfe in the middle with Jill curled at his feet.

Number Five was beside Moya, paws up on the window-sill, giving a little bark of recognition. She patted the dog's head and went downstairs to greet Fyfe. The press reporters ambushed her in front of the reception desk. Camera lights suddenly blazed and radio microphones appeared in front of her face. They didn't all shout at once as they did in films. Instead they waited politely for her to speak. The silence was almost intimidating. Even Number Five was looking up at her expectantly.

'I can confirm that a man's body was found in a nearby cottage last night,' she heard herself saying. 'It is also being treated as murder.'

'Is it related to the woman in white?' a voice asked.

She meant to say possibly but it came out as probably. They all began shouting at once then. In the jumble of words she made out a question about whether she or Fyfe was in charge of the murder inquiry. She bridled.

'I am in charge of this inquiry. I have been from the outset.'

'Were they lovers?'

She blushed furiously, momentarily thinking the question was directed at her and Fyfe.

'How did they die?'

'Is it true someone has already confessed?'

'A confession was made but it was found to be erroneous,' she said. 'Our inquiries are continuing into the manner of the incident. No useful purpose will be served by unverified speculation.'

What did she sound like? They were all shouting at once again. Charlie Simpson opened the dining-room door and grabbed her arm to pull her through. Number Five just made it before the door swung shut on the tip of her tail, making her yelp.

'Dividing line,' Simpson said. 'DCI Fyfe set up a deal that they won't cross it if we feed them information.'

'Has he?'

'Yes. He told them he would speak when he got back from the rock. I doubt if they'll be interested now, not since you've put them straight. You being in charge and all.'

'That's fine then.'

She watched Fyfe step ashore at the jetty. The media pack descended and did to him what they had just done to her.

'Don't worry, Ma'am,' Simpson said. 'They're bound to use you. You're much more photogenic.'

# 33

*Friday, 08.12*

He was waiting for her when she got out of her car on the second floor of the multi-storey beside her office. He came up behind her, tapped her on the shoulder and jumped to one side so that there was no one there when she looked round.

'Surprise,' he said.

Janet Dunbar turned the other way to be confronted by Simon Wright's smiling face. A sense of imminent danger rooted her to the spot. She felt as if she was standing on the edge of a sheer drop and there was no escape from the steady pressure that was pushing her over. She had left Wright hurriedly the night before, after the news of his estranged wife's death had been broken to him. She had been glad to get away and back to her own family, who were collectively slumped in a darkened living-room in front of the television set. They looked up as she opened the door to acknowledge her presence then went back to the film. She went to the bathroom and quietly bounced her head against the wall, cursing herself for ever getting involved with an obvious weirdo.

'You left before we had a chance to decide last night,' he said.

'Decide what?'

'Decide my alibi.'

She had read the morning papers. Laura Lambert, mystic and clairvoyant, was the mysterious lady of Loch Maree found dead on an island in a flowing white robe. Shades of ritual sacrifice and hints of black magic, only slightly detracted from by the suicide pact theory since this guy had been found hanged in a nearby cottage. It said Laura had been dead at least twenty-four hours. That meant she had been killed on Tuesday night. A photograph of her dominated most front pages. She stared accusingly out at Janet who had never seen her before. She really was beautiful.

'Why do you need an alibi?'

'I didn't kill her, Janet.'

'Then why do you need an alibi?'

'To keep the police off my back. I need you to say I was with you on Tuesday night.'

'But you weren't. You didn't turn up.'

'I had business. I need your help. Janet. You'll help me, won't you?'

'What about my family?'

'If you back me up they need never know. It's the way the police work. If they can eliminate me from their inquiries that will be the end of it. There will be no need to take it any further. I know. I'm a lawyer remember.'

'What was the business?'

'When?'

'On Tuesday. What was the business?'

'It was business. Not strictly legal business but certainly nothing like murder. That's why I need your help, Janet.'

'You didn't kill her then?'

'No. I hadn't even seen her for weeks. It was suicide. They found her partner hanging from the rafters.'

'Really.'

'It's true, Janet. It's in the papers. You must trust me.'

Cars swept past on their way up the ramps to other floors. The regular thump of closing doors echoed through the frigid air. Janet was terrified that Wright might be about to grab her by the throat and strangle her. Surely they were in too public a place for that to happen. Yet there was no one around. She could hear the sounds of people but there was no one in sight.

'If you don't back me up our affair is bound to be exposed,' he said. 'Your family will find out. Be my alibi and they need never know. It will save your marriage.'

She bit the knuckle of her index finger and felt herself pushed a few more inches towards the point where she would not be able to stop herself falling. Wright had always frightened her, that had been a big part of the attraction. She had liked it. But now he was frightening her too much.

'It's in your own interests, Janet,' he said. 'I'm not a murderer. If I was, why would I bother arguing with you? Why wouldn't I just kill you too?'

He raised a hand and Janet flinched backwards instinctively. He grinned and reached out slowly to stroke her cheek.

'Tuesday night,' he said. 'You and me. It was a good one, wasn't it?'

Janet nodded weakly.

## 34

*Friday, 09.29*

Eddie Illingworth watched the sand running through the giant hourglass. The bottom bulb was almost half-full now. Grains of sand ran down the sides from the peak of a constantly crumbling pyramid to settle against the glass. The tumbling grains were making a hellish racket, one that thumped and banged inside his head. Only gradually did he realize that the source of the sound was not the hourglass but somewhere else completely. Somebody was hammering on the front door.

They had to hammer on the door because he had disconnected the bell, and taken the telephone off the hook so he wouldn't be disturbed. They had been at it for more than ten minutes. It didn't look as if they were going to give up either. Their perseverance would be rewarded out of Illingworth's curiosity. Whatever it was, he decided, it must be important.

He threw off the covers. The room was like a sauna, hot and airless. His tongue was stuck to the roof of his mouth and left an unpleasant taste when he peeled it free. The first thing he did was light a cigarette and suck some smoke into his lungs. The second thing he did was have a good scratch all over. A bottle of vodka was beside the bed, already watered down and with pieces of orange peel stuffed into the neck to give it a fruity tang. It washed his mouth clean and took the coating off his teeth. He didn't swallow but sprayed it onto the old newspapers stacked in the fireplace.

The knocking had lapsed into a regular pattern, like a morse code message. The volume waxed and waned. He grabbed the boxer shorts hanging on the hourglass and pulled them on as he stumbled out into the corridor. There were three safety chains on the inside of the door, all were hanging loose. The only thing keeping it shut was a flimsy Yale lock. It couldn't be that drastic then or they would have kicked it in by now. Illingworth bent down and picked up a half-smoked cigarette from where it had burned a hole in the carpet. There was lipstick on the tip. He couldn't remember bringing anyone home with him but he checked the rest of the flat, just in case. Then he tossed the fag-end in the toilet and peed on it. Whoever was outside heard the sound of running water and redoubled the hammering.

Illingworth squeezed some toothpaste from a tube and ate it. He went back into the corridor and unlocked the door. His sister Norma stood in front of him with one arm raised as if she was about to throw a spear and a thick bundle of newspapers under the other. She didn't look happy.

'Big sister,' he said, throwing his arms open in mock welcome. 'What a delightful surprise. Forget your keys did you?'

She went straight past him into the kitchen and started banging about, filling the kettle and cutting lumps from a stale loaf of bread to make toast. He followed her and stood in a corner with his arms folded, knowing from long experience that it was not a good idea to try to be clever with her when she was in one of her moods. She obviously wanted to tell him something. He waited patiently for the message to be delivered.

'Good news,' she said with her back to him.

'Good news,' he echoed. 'Always start the day with good news.'

'The good news is you are out of a job.'

'I am.'

She turned to face him. 'Me too. Our owner is dead apparently.'

The shock effect caused more of a buzz in his head than any alcohol he had consumed. 'Ron? Our Ron?'

Norma took hold of her neck with her hands, stuck her tongue out the corner of her mouth, and rolled her eyes until the whites showed.

'You're kidding,' Illingworth said.

She shook her head. The kettle started to get excited and blow steam. 'And there's more.'

'More?'

'Your star columnist, Laura, Princess of Prophecy. She's dead too.'

'Who? Laura?'

'Yes, Laura. She warned you, didn't she?'

'She did?'

'Of course. In her latest column. It was all predicted there.'

'It was?'

'Didn't you read it?'

He had read it but he couldn't actually remember what it said. It had been the usual meaningless guff, quite elegant in its way but full of insubstantial references to life and death and mysterious boatmen and girls on swings. Laura looked forward to her death on the page every month, as far as he was aware. That was what she was paid for, fulfilling her destiny and passing through portals. It went with the territory. Illingworth didn't take any of it seriously. Only the daft subscribers did.

104

And Norma who was sold on the spiritual dimension. She would only work for people with compatible auras. His aura was a bit wonky, she had told him, but he qualified on a genetic basis. She had got him the job on the magazine when no one else would employ him. It didn't mean he had to take it seriously though.

'Was Ron shagging her then?'

'Naturally. Didn't you know?'

He genuinely hadn't realized. He stood, open-mouthed in astonishment until an appreciative smile spread slowly across his face. The bastard was old enough to be her father. If Laura was that desperate he might have had a chance there himself. Who would have prophesied that. Too late now.

He wiped the smile from his face when he noticed Norma's disapproving look. She always seemed to know what he was thinking, but that was one quality he didn't share with her. The female mind was a complete mystery to him. He began to read the accounts of Laura's suicide pact death in the various papers thrown onto the worktop, amusement turning to sympathy as the reality and finality of the deaths sank in. He thought about the trance Norma had been in the day before and her vision of a drowning woman. Laura hadn't drowned but she had been found on this rock in the middle of a loch and then they had dropped the body in the water and been obliged to retrieve her with divers. He wondered if Norma remembered anything about it. He wouldn't tell her if she didn't. It might upset her.

'Get dressed then,' she said.

'Right.'

He went to his bedroom and began to hunt for clothes. He took another swig from the vodka bottle and held it in his mouth for several seconds before swallowing it. He stared at the thin waterfall of sand streaming through the belly of the giant hourglass on the floor beside him. Ron dead. Laura dead. Bloody hell. He wondered if they had been alive when he upturned the hourglass and started the sand running.

'Why am I getting dressed? he shouted.

'To go to the office,' Norma shouted back.

'Why am I going to the office?'

'Because the police will want to see you.'

105

'Why will the police want to see me?'
'Because of what was written in the magazine.'
'But why me?'
'Because you're the editor.'
'So I am.'

# 35

*Friday, 10.32*

'Who are you?'
  'David Fyfe.'
  'Are you a policeman?'
  'That's right.'
  'Where are you taking my mum?'
  'We're going to Edinburgh on an inquiry.'
  'Are you her boss?'
  'Not exactly.'
  'Is she your boss?'
  'Not quite.'
  'What are you then? Just good friends?'
  'Colleagues. That's what we are.'

Isabel McBain had her mother's big eyes and the same quirky little upturn at the corners of her mouth. She was an attractive teenager with long legs, small breasts and ample attitude. She paraded round Fyfe in the living-room of the house studying him as if she was thinking of buying him at an auction sale. Moya was upstairs packing a fresh overnight bag. Fyfe hadn't shaved. He was worried that the dirty tide mark on the collar of his shirt was visible. Combined with his bruised eye he must have resembled some kind of thug or dosser off the street. He ran a hand between shirt collar and neck and sat down in the big armchair.

  'Have a seat,' said Isabel.
  'Thanks.'
  'That's a nasty eye. Did somebody hit you?'

'Yes.'

'Did you hit him back?'

'I didn't get the chance.'

'Did you shoot him?'

'No. He's under arrest now.'

'Did he hit my mum?'

'No.'

'When are you going?'

'Who? Going where?'

'You and mum. To Edinburgh.'

'As soon as possible.'

'What about me?'

'You look as if you're big enough to look after yourself.'

'Appearances can be deceptive.'

'Very true.'

'What's the inquiry?'

'Murder.'

'The bodies at Loch Maree? The one that's in the papers this morning?'

'That's the one.'

'I reckon it's a lover's tiff turned nasty.'

'Do you now? That's what the papers seem to think.'

'A dead man, a dead woman? Together? What do you think?'

'I think appearances can be deceptive.'

Isabel smiled and Fyfe smiled back. Empathy was emerging from the combative cross-examination. She sat opposite him and crossed her legs. She was wearing tight jeans and a loose T-shirt with a tiger pattern on it. A thin black silk scarf was tied round her throat. 'Don't even start to think about it,' Fyfe told himself silently. He looked round the room so that he wouldn't have to look at her. It was tastefully furnished, feminine flourishes everywhere.

'How long will mum be away?'

'A couple of days perhaps.'

'Are you her boss?'

'You've asked me that already.'

'I only got a wishy-washy reply. Are you her boss? You can tell me. I can take it.'

'Actually, she's my boss in this inquiry.'

'Is she now? How do you feel about taking orders from a woman?'

'Depends what the orders are.'

'Good answer. Are you going to arrest somebody?'

'Hopefully.'

'Will you use guns?'

'I doubt it.'

'Why not?'

'No need.'

'But he's a murderer?'

'How do you know it's a he?'

'I jump to conclusions.'

'I thought you might.'

'Do you know who you are going to arrest?'

'Not yet.'

'How did they die?'

'She was bashed on the head. He was hanging from the rafters.'

'I told you. Star-crossed lovers.'

'Suppose that's what somebody wants us to think.'

'Smart. Who?'

'The real murderer.'

'And that's why you're going to Edinburgh?'

'Correct.'

'To find him.'

'When you grow up you should join the police force like your mum.'

'I'm going to be an accountant. There's more money in it.'

'Clever girl.'

'I take after my mum.'

'You could do worse.'

Moya came into the room carrying a bulky shoulder bag. The short skirt had been replaced by a pair of plain black trousers. Isabel's presence seemed to give her an air of maternal well-being that contrasted with the brisk efficiency of the person at the loch that morning who had set up and delegated all the routine investigative and forensic tasks before informing Fyfe they were heading south. He stood up and offered to take her bag.

'You've met my daughter then?'

'Charming girl. Just like her mum.'

'God, I hope not. You'll be all right on your own for a few days, won't you Isabel?'

'Oh, I think I might survive. The big question is will you be all right in the care of your colleague.'

She was looking straight at Fyfe. When he bent down to pick up the bag he got the impression the two women were winking at each other across his back. He fingered the collar of his shirt again as he straightened up and followed Moya out. In the driveway he loaded the bag into the back of the Volvo. The dogs pressed their noses against the glass.

'Nice colour,' Isabel said, wrinkling her nose and touching the purple paint with a fingertip as though it was red hot.

'I chose it to go with my damaged eye.'

Fyfe acted the gentleman opening the passenger door for Moya. She slipped in and wound down the window.

'No wild parties.'

'Same to you.'

'No boyfriends staying the night.'

'Same to you.'

'Be good.'

'Same to you.'

'And if you can't be good be careful.'


# 36


*Friday, 11.27*


Douglas Lambert looked down on the face of his dead daughter and wondered why he couldn't cry. It had been the same with his wife Lorraine, her face all withered and shrunken from illness. And again with his own teenage son Tony, not a mark on the outside of his shattered body when they cut him free from the mangled wreckage of the car crash. There were no tears, just an overwhelming sense of sadness that was like a drug injected directly into his veins. The grief soothed him. It didn't matter what she had done to him, how she had treated him. She was his daughter and he would never see her again after this moment. The grief insulated him from the ordinary world and allowed him to function normally so that no-one would ever guess that he was the victim of bereavement.

The police had been predictable. An apology, a brief explanation, a sense of compassion, a cup of hot sweet tea. The three of them had handled it well. Their training had been thorough. Their concern seemed genuine. They were patient and understanding, aware that there was no formula reaction to the news of bereavement. Its effect was unpredictable, sometimes weakening the strong, at other times strengthening the weak. The death of a child can kill a human personality, and a son or daughter is always a child no matter how old they grow.

Lambert had seen it so often in the course of his work. It was the change in the eyes of the stricken parents. The emptiness that yawned on ultimate realization, like stepping off a cliff and standing there, cartoon-style, before plummeting down. It had happened to him with his son several days after his death. Laura had never forgiven him for the death of her brother. That was when everthing between them had changed. He was still falling.

Pat had been warm and comforting, taking the edge off his grief, and her own, by inviting him into her bed. They were able to talk dispassionately about the possibility that her husband might have been having a love affair with his daughter, and both decided to agree it hadn't happened. It was easier that way. It may have been the obvious interpretation but it was the wrong one, Lambert insisted and Pat took comfort from his certainty. The newspapers had jumped on it as an explanation but they didn't know half the real story. A report on the radio said that relatives (that was them) were travelling north to confirm the identities of the young woman and the middle-aged man found dead at Loch Maree.

They had driven to Inverness on the near-empty early morning roads. Old friends didn't have to talk much. No point in blaming themselves for the actions of others. The full story would come out soon enough. Their own affair was discreet, unsuspected and unconnected. Every now and then they exchanged a look of mutual understanding, but not a word was spoken.

The mortuary was familiar territory for Lambert. He had collected many bodies there for their last journey south. He recognized the staff without knowing their names. They were good, professional in their approach. No undue delay. He was led one way, Pat another. He stood over his daughter's body and they pulled back the cover to reveal her face. The injury to the side of her head marred her looks. Her hair was matted around it, crusty blood forming into crooked rats'-tails. The post-mortem would make it worse, but it could easily be put right afterwards.

He could have her made beautiful again. It wouldn't be difficult. He wouldn't do it himself, not to one of his own, but it was a great comfort to him that the capability existed to ensure that Laura would sleep pretty in her final resting place.

He had once had a premonition about Laura's death. He had never told anybody. It was not recent, but long ago, on the day of her eighth birthday. There had been a party with all her friends in pretty dresses and presents and a cake. By the evening she was exhausted and barely able to walk. He had carried her through to her bedroom and gently undressed her before slipping her into bed. He lay down beside her for a few minutes, aware of the warmth of her body and the small movement of her breathing. It was a stormy summer day outside, still light with torn clouds flying across the sky. He kissed her forehead and wondered at the miracle of the growing child, growing and developing. She could not be a child for ever as his dead son would be. Lambert realized then instinctively that little Laura would die before him. She would grow up and she would die and he would look down on her lifeless body. Nothing surer. It was guaranteed. How sad and how satisfying to be proved right.

# 37

Simon Wright, the lady in the loch's estranged husband, sat on the edge of his chair in the bare interview room. He kept one hand spread on the table and the other on his knee. He was wearing a grey suit with a red and yellow patterned waistcoat and matching tie. The bright colours clashed with the paleness of his face and the glow of the overhead light on his balding scalp. He retained a semblance of the oily good looks of his youth. He had a flat stomach and broad chest but close up you could see the insidious damage time had inflicted.

Pleasantries had already been exchanged and the bare bones of the morning's press reports padded out with the nasty little details next of kin are entitled to know. The table had a large tape recorder on it and wires disappeared into the wall beneath an integral four-foot square mirror which unsubtly suggested there was someone in a room on the other side watching. Fyfe was on the other side, watching Moya question Wright. The tape was running though it wasn't needed. Wright had come in voluntarily, declining the presence of a lawyer because he used to be one himself and knew the rules of the game.

Fyfe remembered him from way back. The kind who turned up at the cells at short notice to bail out the kind of crook who racked up convictions for dishonesty the way other people got parking tickets. Eventually, several years ago now, he had abandoned the law as a loss leader and gone into business himself. No convictions yet. Matthewson stood behind Moya with his hands clasped behind his back. He appeared to be looking over her shoulder to get a better view of her legs. Maybe Fyfe wasn't the only one finding it difficult to concentrate. She had been relaxed and friendly during their trip south, had thought it a great idea to stay in Fyfe's empty flat rather than go through the rigmarole of getting authorization for a hotel. By the time they reached the Forth Bridge Fyfe was rather regretting the fact that they had a lot of time-consuming work to do. There was more to life than bringing murderers to justice.

'It's good of you to come in to see us, Mr Wright.'

'I have to tell you Inspector,' Wright said. 'My attitude in these matters is to be scrupulously honest.'

'Very refreshing,' Moya replied.

'I know how the police work so there is no point in my trying to mislead or obstruct you in any way.'

'Good. Then no one's time will be wasted. When did you last see your wife, Mr Wright?'

'Three weeks ago this morning.'

'You recall it exactly?'

'I do.'

'Why is that?'

'We met to discuss our divorce arrangements and what to do with mutual insurance policies.'

'And what did you decide?'

'That I should continue paying premiums on the life insurance we held and that they should be converted to single life policies.'

'The single life being Laura's?'

'Yes.'

'Payable on her death?'

'Yes.'

'Is it a substantial sum?'

'Four policies amounting to eight hundred thousand pounds.'

'Eight hundred thousand pounds?'

'Yes. I doubled the amount three weeks ago because they fell for renewal and I exploited the opportunity.'

'You're bloody right you did.'

'It seemed like the thing to do. Increases could be made without charge and without recourse to medical examination. I guess I was just lucky.'

'Your wife seems to have had the bad luck, doesn't she?'

Behind the mirror, Fyfe folded his arms and shook his head at Moya's impetuosity. Matthewson raised his eyebrows at the mirror and rose a little off his heels in body language straight out of Donald McIsaac's repertoire. If he had bent at the knees and snapped his braces Fyfe would not have been surprised.

He had to admire Wright's brazen approach. No apologetic admission. No shamefaced murmurings or expressions of regret. Bumping up your insurance a few weeks before the death of your spouse might look bad to suspicious minds but that was just the way it was. Of course, Wright knew full well his finances would be checked out to see if he had profited from Laura's death. He would never have been able to hide it. So he used it to his advantage. Had it taped at his own request. Would my client have acted in such a way if he intended to kill his wife, the QC would argue at the trial. Good question. Think about it ladies and gentlemen of the jury.

'You will inherit eight hundred thousand pounds as a result of your wife's death?' Moya asked rhetorically.

'I will,' Wright answered unnecessarily.

'That's an awful lot of money.'

'It is. The premiums were quite heavy too.'

'You haven't had to pay them for very long.'

'That is the nature of insurance. It is to allow for the unexpected. You are insured, aren't you Inspector?'

'Maybe,' Moya snapped.

'You are very wise to be insured. Everybody's future is uncertain.'

'Yours looks pretty assured now.'

'Naturally, I will allow a decent interval before I collect the money.'

Moya was getting flustered. Fyfe could see the colour rising in her cheeks. Her eyes flashed threateningly. She fidgeted on her seat, making her blouse crease endearingly where it was tucked into the top of her trousers. He could just see a nicely turned ankle round the side of the table. Matthewson was looking at the ankle too. So was Wright, before lifting his gaze to meet Moya's. He had that little half-smile on his lips all crooked lawyers wear on their faces when they are sure of themselves. Go on, it invited. Do your worst. I am an expert at playing games with the legal system.

114

Wright held up a hand and studied the palm for ages before looking back across at Moya. Fyfe leaned closer to the far side of the one-way mirror so he didn't miss any of the game. He felt the light stubble on his chin. He would definitely need to shave soon.

'Can you account for your movements earlier this week?' Moya asked.

Wright crossed his legs and sighed. 'Last night I was in the office all day and had dinner with a friend at my home. Wednesday was another full day in the office and I had a ticket for the Hearts game at Tynecastle.'

'Who was playing?'

'Kilmarnock.'

'What was the score?'

'Three nil to Hearts. I was in one of the executive boxes so there are plenty of witnesses. I stayed for two hours after the end of the game enjoying the hospitality, then I got a taxi home.'

'Tuesday?'

'Tuesday was the office again and later I met my girlfriend. We had sex at my house and I ran her home around eleven.'

'Run that by me again, will you.'

'I am having an affair with a married woman. We were together on Tuesday night.'

'We'll need her name.'

'Of course. I would appreciate it if you would contact her at work. There is no need for her family to know about this. She will be very anxious for this to be dealt with sensitively.'

'I'm sure she would.'

Back off the bastard, Fyfe advised silently through the mirror as he saw Moya's face harden. He's got the upper hand for the moment. Don't give him the satisfaction of seeing how frustrated you are. Back off until we can find something to use against him.

Matthewson butted in. 'When did you last see your girlfriend?'

'Last night. She was there when you arrived to tell me about Laura. She hid in the kitchen.'

'You'll forgive me for mentioning it Mr Wright, but you don't seem very cut up about your wife's death? You didn't last night either.'

'We don't all have to wear our emotions on our sleeves, you know detective. I was very fond of Laura but we were separated for quite some time and my emotions are now engaged elsewhere. I feel a great degree of sadness at her death but I am not totally devastated. That may seem harsh but that's just the way I'm made.'

'You don't seem very surprised either.'

'Nothing Laura did ever surprised me. She was a cruel bitch, viciously cruel, only really interested in herself. That was partly the reason for our separation. Don't ask me to cry alligator tears.'

'Crocodile.'

'Pardon?'

'The expression describing an insincere show of emotion is crocodile tears.'

'Crocodiles then.'

Moya stood up and all attention in the room fixed on her. 'Did you know about her affair with Ron Gilchrist?'

'No. Did he kill her?'

'Did you know him?'

'Vaguely. Very vaguely.'

'Did she have other lovers?'

'Huh.'

The unintelligible noise was unexpectedly loud, an explosive exclamation that filled the room and bounced off the mirror. Behind it Fyfe jerked his head back. Wright uncrossed his legs and placed both hands in front of himself on the table.

'Do I interpret that as a yes?' Moya asked.

'Yes.'

'Names?'

'No names, just bodies. I didn't want to know.'

'Somebody called Robert perhaps?'

'Robert? No. Maybe. I don't know.'

Fyfe saw vulnerability pass over Wright like a cloud over the sun. His vanity was hurt that Laura should prefer other men to him. Murders had been committed for less. Moya hit him when

116

he was down by tossing the proof copy of *Ethereal* magazine onto the table.

'Do you believe in the supernatural Mr Wright?' Moya said.

'Not really. I do read my horoscope most days.'

'Funny to have a wife in the business and not be a believer.'

'Laura didn't believe. It was her living that's all. She was a fraud.'

'Was she?'

'Of course. She would probably admit it herself if you asked her. Only the impressionable and the inadequate were taken in.'

'Is that so? She couldn't see into the future then?'

'No. I don't think so.'

'Have you read her latest column in the magazine? It's not officially published until Monday, by the way. But that won't stop us. You can read it now.'

'I never read her stupid column. It's a heap of nonsense.'

'Maybe so but you should read this one. Go on.'

Wright's self-confidence had gone shaky. He was wishing he had never started this confrontation now that he was on the receiving end. Curiosity made him frown unhappily. He picked up the magazine reluctantly and stared into the disembodied eyes on the cover.

'Page sixteen,' Moya said.

Wright turned to the page and began reading. Fyfe and Moya and Matthewson studied him intently as he absorbed the words. His face was a picture, heating up to bright pink at the mid-way point and then fading to ash grey as he read through to the end. Once he turned to the cover to check the date and once he looked up at Moya as the significance dawned on him. She smiled the kind of little half-smile police officers allow themselves when they succeed in wrong-footing smart villains.

'The future is with us now, Mr Wright,' Moya said. 'Laura can't be here to tell us herself but it looks as if she left us a few clues.'

## 38

*Friday, 14.54*

Fyfe and Moya ate a pub lunch in an old-fashioned pub where the barmen wore chest-high white aprons and narrow beams of sunlight poked through the clear bits of the stained glass windows like the triggers for a sophisticated electronic alarm system. They walked through the unavoidable lattice of beams to a corner booth and chewed over the possibility of Wright's guilt or innocence. With the cockiness knocked out of him, he had been released and cautioned to stay available. Matthewson had got the name of his girlfriend and been delegated to check up on him more thoroughly. He wasn't invited for lunch.

The offices of *Ethereal* magazine were ten minutes' walk away from the pub on the top floor of a short, run-down terrace where the buildings seemed to be held together by blue and white To Let signs. There were two rooms; a large outer one with four paper-cluttered desks and two big computer screens, and the editor's cubby hole behind flimsy panels and three tall panes of frosted glass. The toilet at the top of three flights of stairs was shared with a firm of insurance brokers on the other side of the landing. The small windows looked out over rubbish-strewn back gardens and long disused rusty clothes-poles onto the rear of another terrace opposite. To the front was an uninspiring cobbled street streaked with lengths of tarmac and another unbroken row of identical buildings. The surroundings were as dowdy as the magazine was glossy.

After climbing the stairs they were met at the door by Eddie Illingworth who led them across the outer room to his interior office. Space was so limited by the jumble of filing cabinets and book-crammed shelves it was difficult for Fyfe to stop his leg touching Moya's as they sat together and introductions were exchanged. He didn't try too hard.

Illingworth looked dreadful. His skin was waxen, his eyes bloodshot, and his unkempt greying hair exploded in clumps from his head. Each sentence he spoke was ended by an unhealthy cough that seemed to cause him a stab of pain. He shifted nervously and constantly in a chair that creaked loudly beneath him. An incipient alcoholic if ever there was a stereotype for one. Fyfe felt sorry for him.

'How's business?' Moya asked.

'On the up. Interest in the unknown is a nice earner at the moment, but who knows what will happen now that Ron's dead.'

'You know that Mr Gilchrist is dead then?'

'Eh, yes.' He twisted and writhed in the noisy chair. 'Isn't that why you're here?'

'Who told you Mr Gilchrist was dead?'

'It's in the papers. My sister Norma showed me them. She works here too. She's the organized one. I'll get her. She should be around somewhere. Hang on a minute.'

Illingworth got up and pushed past the two of them to get to the door. A blast of mint-flavoured breath freshener convinced Fyfe that he had already been drinking that morning. They heard him go outside and shout Norma's name down the stairs. Then he returned and squeezed back into his chair, more nervous than ever. He played with a ruler, bending it dangerously close to breaking point in a curve between his hands.

'She just popped out,' he explained. 'I'm sure she'll be back soon.'

'Your sister?' Fyfe said.

'We're a very close family. We've got to give each other jobs. No one else will. You'll like Norma. She's very funny. Has a talent for mimicry. If she wasn't so shy she would go far in showbiz.'

'Who is Pat?' Moya asked.

'Pat is Ron's wife. She works here as advertising manager and general dogsbody. He bought the magazine for her, if you want to know the truth. She must know about this too, I suppose. You would tell her, wouldn't you? Before the papers got hold of it.'

119

Moya nodded encouragingly. The curve of the ruler slackened slightly. Illingworth coughed and his rib cage took as much punishment as the creaking chair.

'You will know that Laura Lambert is dead too.'

'Suicide pact the papers say.'

'Do you believe it?'

'She was a bit dippy.'

'Dippy?'

'And Ron was a true dewy-eyed romantic. So it's possible.'

'Were you aware that the owner of this magazine was having an affair with one of your columnists?'

'No, I certainly wasn't. I work in glorious seclusion up here. There's Pat and Norma and a couple of temporaries we take on in pre-press week. All the commissioning of articles is done by phone and seventy per cent of the pages are adverts anyway. I never saw Laura for months on end. She just fired in her column on computer disk. There were never any problems with her. Never missed a deadline yet.'

'And Mr Gilchrist?'

'He was in regularly. He liked to keep an eye on all the admin and stuff but it was really Pat who ran it day to day. We were making a healthy profit, you know.'

'What do you make of Laura's latest column?'

'What do you mean?'

'Its content I mean,' Moya said. 'Doesn't it surprise you?'

A puzzled expression became one of pain as Illingworth turned his head to one side to let a cough out. He put down the ruler and picked a stapled proof copy of the magazine from one of his drawers. He turned to the correct page and began to read. Moya looked at Fyfe and then back at Illingworth waiting for his reaction. Fyfe snatched a sly glance at her ankles.

'Not bad,' Illingworth said after a few minutes. 'The island in the middle of the loch and all that.' Realization of the significance dawned on him suddenly. 'It's incredible. That's where she was found, isn't it?'

'What's the matter, Mr Illingworth?' Moya said. 'Why should it surprise you? Don't you believe in the power of prophecy?'

Illingworth sat back in his chair and genuinely relaxed for the first time since they had sat down in front of him. 'Do me a favour, will you. This is just a job. *Was* a job, rather, now that Ron's dead. God knows what will happen here with him six feet under.'

'You should sign him up from beyond the grave,' Fyfe said. 'After all you've lost your princess of prophecy.'

Moya kicked him gently in the shin. 'When would this column have been written, Mr Illingworth?' she continued.

'Weeks ago probably. Norma organized it every month. She was always the point of contact with Laura.'

'But when is the latest deadline?'

'Seven days before print day.'

'Which was?'

'Tuesday was print day, so the Tuesday before. The finished glossies will be ready for distribution today.'

'When Laura Lambert was very much alive and kicking.'

'If you say so, but I rather think if you read some of our back numbers you'll find some equally bizarre predictions that never came true. This one was just lucky.'

'Exactly,' Fyfe said.

Illingworth shifted uncomfortably and creakily in his chair. 'I'll get you a bundle of old mags,' he muttered.

'You're not a psychic yourself then, Mr Illingworth?' Moya asked.

'No. I leave that to my staff and contributors. I just give the readers what they want. I'm a professional in the here and now. Presentation, snappy headlines, quality lay-out. The hereafter is a closed shop to me but I'll make one prediction if you want.'

'What?'

'The publicity over the murders will make this issue a sell-out.' He sat up, enlivened by the prospect as it occurred to him. 'It might even attract a new buyer. I might not be out of a job after all. Pat might carry on too.'

'Always a bright side, eh Eddie?' Fyfe said.

'What about Mr Gilchrist?' Moya persisted. 'Was he into mysticism and the like?'

'You could say that. Definitely a bit other-worldly but he put his money where his spiritual being hovered and was making a substantial profit out of it, so he can't have been that daft.'

'Laura Lambert?'

'Oh yes. She was a real weirdo. Certified. Category one. She used to be on the telly, you know. It didn't last.'

'We know.'

'She wasn't weird in a careless way. She knew what she was about. When she got chucked off the telly she turned to mail-order fortune telling and psychic consultations.'

'Very commendable.'

'I thought she was good. Good writer too. She provoked floods of letters every month.'

'Her husband seems to think she was a fraud.'

'Never met her husband. I've heard he's a right bastard. Mind you, she could probably give as good as she got. She was a tough lady. I wouldn't like to get on the wrong side of her.'

'Ever meet any of her boyfriends? An attractive woman like that with a broken marriage was bound to have more than one admirer.'

'No. I had absolutely no idea Ron was poking her. Honest. He never let on.'

'Any reason why he should?'

'What? Poke her?'

'Tell you?'

'No.'

'You weren't, were you?'

'What?'

'Poking her? She was a good-looking woman.'

'Who? Me? Laura? I'd have liked to but she was way out of my league. I didn't have the money or the stamina.'

'Do you know anyone called Robert?'

'Lots of people probably.'

'Anyone who might have known Laura and was called Robert?'

'I don't think so.'

Illingworth wiped his nose and shook his head. He began to bend the ruler again. The outer door of the office opened. Moya and Fyfe looked round and saw an out-of-focus shape cross the floor and approach the frosted windows.

'That will be Norma back,' Illingworth said, standing up. 'She'll be able to give you a better insight into the characters in this drama. She handled Laura and most of our other writers. If it wasn't for Norma keeping us all on the straight and narrow nothing would ever appear in print.'

The door opened and Patricia Gilchrist entered. She looked as if she was about to shout at Illingworth but hesitated at the sight of strangers. Fyfe stood up and nodded in greeting.

'Oh, it's you, Pat. We were just talking about the future of the mag. Laura's last column is likely to make it a best-seller.'

Pat laughed with dismissive sarcasm. 'Laura never wrote a column in her life.'

Illingworth collapsed back into his chair. Moya rose beside Fyfe and turned to face the newcomer. 'Who did then?' she asked.

'Norma, of course. She always produced the words and Laura always took the credit.' She laughed again. 'They worked well together.'

# 39

*Friday, 15.30*

Eddie Illingworth sat outside while police took over his office to speak to Pat Gilchrist. He fiddled with a computer terminal and started a beat 'em up game from the hard disk, taking on the persona of a battle-hardened jungle commando rescuing hostages held by a cunning and numerically superior enemy. He died twice before he got past the first booby trap and adjusted the sound level of the electronic death screams in case they disturbed his visitors.

On the other side of the opaque glass he watched the three ill-defined shapes. The woman with the nice legs had taken his seat, Pat Gilchrist had taken her seat in front of the desk and the bloke Fyfe was standing behind her beside the door.

Illingworth retrieved another ammo clip and tossed a couple of grenades ahead. The enemy on the screen died with far-off, near-inaudible squeaks of pain.

He must have looked a bit of an idiot, he supposed, not

realizing that his magazine's star columnist didn't actually write the material that went under her name. It didn't matter in a sense, but Norma might have given him a hint about what was going on. She had never harboured any ambition to be a writer as far as he was aware. What was the big secret? Or maybe it wasn't a secret. Maybe he was the only one not to know. What other tales was Pat telling them about Ron and Laura? What else was going to emerge that he didn't know about? Maybe he should phone some of his contacts to see if there were any jobs going. He didn't know that many people any more. They were either dead or sacked or retired from the rat race and growing potatoes on distant crofts.

His patched-up heart skipped a beat and he coughed, spraying the screen with spittle as a whole platoon of the enemy were taken out by a shoulder-held rocket launcher. He wiped it dry with his sleeve and winced in empathy as a volley of machine-gun bullets thumped into him and blood splashed from his *alter ego*. His life-meter shrank abruptly to below fifty per cent.

Where was Norma? Her out-of-body experience on Thursday morning had provided her with a vision of a white-clad woman floating on the water. Then Laura was found on an island in the middle of a loch and a piece in the magazine, written by Laura at least two weeks previously, described the same thing. Where was Norma? What had she done? Illingworth felt very cold. His hands had stopped moving on the keyboard. On the computer screen his life-meter was down to ten per cent and flashing a warning. He licked his dry lips and anticipated a soothing drink.

Pat was walking past him, saying goodbye. She would contact him soon about the future. The woman policeman went too, leaving Fyfe standing beside him handing him a card from his wallet.

'If your sister is in contact with you we would be very interested to hear from her,' he said. 'Phone me on this number. Any time.'

Illingworth opened the card and handed over the half dozen copies of old magazines he had got ready. Fyfe followed the two women out the door. Oh my God, Illingworth was thinking, what has my sweet sister done? What has she done? Being psychic wouldn't be much of a defence if they charged the silly lassie with murder. Surely not? Murder? Double murder? Not Norma? His little sister? Did she really have it in her?

On the screen the enemy attacked and his life-meter fell to zero. You have been terminated, the screen announced in vivid red letters. He died and the unequal game ended with a long drawn-out, whispering scream.

# 40

*Friday, 16.45*

A whole new dimension to the case was opened by Pat Gilchrist's version of events. According to her, Norma and Laura were lesbian lovers involved in a torrid affair. Norma must have planned the murder, sketching out the details in the column she ghosted. Poor, stupid, love-struck Ron was part of the plan. He had somehow been lured to the murder scene and killed so that the finger of blame would point at him.

'It makes sense and explains a lot if it's true,' Moya said as they walked the dogs on Corstorphine Hill after dropping Pat off at her home. 'We've gone full circle back to the crime of passion.'

She was totally convinced. Fyfe could see it in her manner, though she wasn't going to be too assertive about it after the débâcle of the Robert Ross episode. He wasn't going to remind her of that or of the new evidence the team had found up there of a distinctive tyre mark in the mud of the forest track outside the cottage. It was the impression of an s-shaped cut in the tread and it was found underneath Gilchrist's Range Rover so it couldn't have been made by any of the police vehicles. Of course, it might turn out to be totally innocent, a Post Office van or anything like that. It would be checked out.

Fyfe sat on the bonnet of the car leafing through the old magazines. He kicked a stone and Number Five went scampering after it. They had already tried Norma's home address. No one at home and now little brother Eddie had disappeared too. An arrest warrant for Norma was being prepared.

'Cold-blooded passion too,' Moya went on. 'If we take into account that nasty Norma planned the whole thing a couple of weeks in advance.'

'Try a couple of months in advance,' Fyfe said. 'Listen to this from the princess of prophecy in last month's magazine: *And I shall die surrounded by my handmaidens, the water birds, under a vast sky with the coldness lapping at my face and the ferryman fading into the mist.*'

'Let me see that,' Moya demanded, taking the magazine.

Fyfe opened another copy and bent the cover back on itself. 'From the month before: *I shall be placed in the centre and my atoms will merge with elemental forces once the boat's final journey is complete. Death will welcome me and justice will be done.* A certain similarity in tone and content, don't you think?'

'She was planning it for ages, screwing up her courage to be able to do it. Once Laura was dead she knew exactly what she was going to do with her.'

'Doesn't mean she bumped her off. What's her motive?'

'Lover's quarrel? Insanity? Perhaps she thought Laura was too good for this world so she helped her pass into the next one. Perhaps Laura thought so too and asked for her help. We're dealing with serious dreamers who are not of our world here. It's not exactly rational to lay out your murder victim on a slab for public viewing.'

'An element of exhibitionism there.'

'Almost as if the murderer wanted to be caught.'

'Or wanted the body to be found so he could brazen it out and collect his insurance money.'

'The way things are going slimy Simon may be off the hook and home free with his windfall. He might be psychic and not even know it.'

'Pity,' Fyfe said with feeling. 'What about Ron Gilchrist? Was he just a convenient fall-guy then?'

'If we're to believe the grieving widow.'

'And do we?'

The dogs were running about on the periphery of Fyfe's

vision and Moya was standing directly in front of him. He could have reached out, caught her in his arms and pulled her in against him. The urge to kiss her and squeeze her tightened like a cramp in his shoulders and at the back of his knees. She was smiling at him delightfully. He just managed to stop himself.

'I'm remembering what you taught me yesterday,' Moya said.

'What was that?'

'Not to jump to conclusions.'

'Aha. The first law of prophecy; the most obvious conclusion is likely to be the wrong one.'

'And the most likely outcome is one that nobody anticipates.'

'Which means we're no further forward really.'

'Not until we find nasty Norma we're not.'

'We still don't know who this bloody Bobby guy is?'

'No. He doesn't fit in at all, does he?'

Moya put her hands on her hips underneath her jacket and took a deep breath. Fyfe rubbed his knee and complained obliquely about an ancient sports injury.

'What now then?' he said.

'We've still to see Laura's father, the undertaker.'

'You can ask him if he knew his daughter was a dyke.'

'Thanks very much.'

'You're the boss.'

# 41

*Friday, 17.26*

Matthewson swept all the messages written on bits of yellow sticky paper into the bin. He sat down thankfully and peeled a banana. An afternoon of trudging round trying to dig some decent dirt on Simon Wright had been a waste of time. His alibi had checked out so far. He had been at Tynecastle for the football on Wednesday. If he stuck to his story he was bullet-proof and a lot richer with the insurance money. A request for information from the insurance company was currently running the gauntlet of bureaucracy. Matthewson put his feet up on the desk and bit the top off the banana, imagining it was Wright's head.

The phone rang. Matthewson would have liked to, but he couldn't copy Fyfe's party trick of ignoring it. His curiosity was always too great. To him every ring was a maddening itch demanding to be scratched. One day, he fondly believed, he would answer a call and it would change his life. At the very least it might give him the lead needed to crack a case and show up his superiors. He stuffed the rest of the banana into his mouth, picked up the receiver and found himself unable to speak for several seconds while he chewed and swallowed.

'Detective Sergeant Matthewson,' he said at last.

'This is Janet Dunbar. You left a message at my office.'

Her voice sounded timid and frightened, as if she would be scared away by the slightest thing. He lowered his feet slowly to the floor and hunched over, cradling the phone protectively. He would have to treat this situation very delicately. Somehow he had expected a more strident character to match Wright's up front personality.

'Mrs Dunbar. I need to see you,' he said.

'I realize that.'

'I don't want to cause you any inconvenience or embarrassment but it is necessary that I talk to you.'

'Yes,' she said. 'I took the afternoon off. I had to have some time to myself.'

'You know why I want to see you?'

'It's about the murders at the loch, isn't it? The woman and the man.'

'That's right. I understand you're a friend of . . .'

She wasn't listening to him. Her voice was steadily rising in pitch, bordering on hysteria.

'My boyfriend's your murderer,' she said. 'He used to be married to the dead woman. He killed her.'

Matthewson balled his hand into a fist and punched the air. So much for a rock-solid alibi, he thought. He would get this firmed up and present it to DCI Fyfe and DI McBain who, as far as he knew, were out indulging in their own personal extracurricular activities. He would solve the crime and take the credit.

'I didn't know what to do,' she said. 'I'm married, you see. I have children. Can you help me?'

'Of course. Where are you? I'll come round.'

## 42

*Friday, 19.02*

The reporters had made the family connection and were now camped outside Lambert's funeral parlour. He could watch them watching him by crouching and lifting the bottom edge of the window-blind to look down from his first floor flat above the shop. They were in the same pair of cars that had been parked in Pat's street, the same squirrel-cheeked fat man was squashed in behind the steering-wheel of the lead car chain-smoking and drinking coffee from a regular supply of polystyrene cups bought at the corner shop. The street was busy with slanting tables of fruit and vegetables occupying enough pavement space to slow down the steady stream of people in both directions. The street where he had lived for more than ten years looked strange to him. He had never studied it in any great detail before, never looked at the garish shop signs, and the torn awnings, and the bunches of wires than ran up walls like bulging veins, and the dirty windows of empty flats over the shops, and the thin stalks of plants growing from the muck accumulated over years in the roof gutters. He had never previously taken any notice of the huge illuminated advertisement hoarding in the gap site directly opposite. It changed every twenty seconds, slats revolving from an abstract nude for Silk Cut cigarettes, to a giant jar of Nescafé, to a luxury Toyota car throwing up a dust-cloud against a desert background, and full circle again to Silk Cut's disjointed nakedness.

Lambert wasn't going to give the bloody reporters what they

wanted. He wasn't going to break down in tears and lament the passing of his only daughter in neat quotable sentences. He wasn't going to get the photograph album out to find some nice cute shots of Laura as a little girl for them to publish. 'Come on, Mr Lambert,' they had shouted to him. 'Deal with us and we'll go away and leave you alone.' On the contrary he would leave them well alone. Let them rot.

He dropped the blind and retreated to his favourite armchair. He was drunk. Half a bottle of brandy had vanished since Pat had left him, her anger driving itself like a wedge between them as she turned events over in her mind and came to the conclusion that maybe her husband Ron wasn't the pathetic old fool she imagined but instead an intelligent, scheming adulterer with a death wish.

Lambert couldn't realistically challenge her. His whole crazy idea had been to make her believe exactly that. He couldn't tell her the truth. He couldn't tell anyone the truth now. It was sealed into its own coffin and would be buried as soon as possible. A funeral for the truth. Not too many mourners would attend.

The intercom buzzed. Lambert heaved himself out of the chair and went over to the speaker by the door. John Bannister, the deputy manager downstairs, informed him the police had arrived. Lambert told him to send them up. He could put up two fingers to the press but it would be stupid not to get the police on his side. The pre-funeral formalities would not take long. He unlocked the door.

There were two of them, an attractive woman and a seedy-looking man with a badly bruised eye. They introduced themselves and showed identification but the names did not register in Lambert's head. They said how sorry they were that Laura was dead. He slumped back in his chair and apologized for being drunk, tacitly demanding understanding as a grieving parent, openly promising co-operation, secretly wishing they would go away and leave him in self-pitying peace.

'Have you any idea who might have killed your daughter,' the woman detective asked while the man moved about the room, unsettling him.

130

'Laura?' he said, without quite knowing why. As if there was any doubt about her being his daughter.

'Of course. Do you have any idea who might have killed her?'

Lambert shook his head.

'Have you any idea who might have killed Ron Gilchrist? I believe he was a friend of yours?'

'Yes. No idea. I've been thinking it was a suicide after he killed Laura.'

'No. This remains a murder inquiry Mr Lambert.'

'You mean it wasn't suicide?'

'We have evidence that indicates otherwise.'

'For Ron as well? Is it what Pat's been telling you?'

'No. It's objective evidence which will be confirmed by the postmortem results.'

'I see. So it's not just Pat then?'

A horrible, gut-churning feeling of helplessness came over Lambert. The bile rose in his throat and, bursting like the skin of an over-stretched bubble, caused a sudden repellent taste to fill his mouth. He drank some brandy and loosened the leash on a little more of his self-control. It had been a stupid idea from the first. It had never had a chance of succeeding. His eyes watered and the room went out of focus. The woman detective's shape swam across his blurred vision and patted his knee. He should have known it would never work.

'It must be a difficult time for you, Mr Lambert, but it would assist us greatly if you would just answer a few questions.'

'Of course, of course.' He wiped his eyes, drank more brandy. 'Is it true you begin to notice your surroundings more acutely just before you die?'

'Perhaps.'

'But only if you know you are going to die?'

Moya patted his knee again, trying to gain his attention. 'There are things we have been told about your daughter, Mr Lambert. We need to know if they are accurate.'

'I'm a respectable man. You can't get much more respectable than an undertaker. People trust you with their dead. You seal their loved ones in their boxes and lay them in their last resting places. You've got to be trustworthy for people to let you do

131

that. I'm so respectable. Look at me. Strictly orthodox. Respectability personified.'

The male detective sat beside him on the arm of the chair. A warning sounded in Lambert's mind. He drank more brandy to dull it. He was raving. He shouldn't talk so much. He might let something slip out.

'Laura must have been a bit of an embarrassment to a respectable man then? What with her clairvoyance and her fortune-telling and all the New Age philosophy stuff.'

'That didn't bother me. It was just a bit of fun.'

'Ron Gilchrist too as a family friend. Running that weird magazine.'

'It was always Pat's magazine. He indulged her and it made money anyway. Ron would have published anything as long as it made money.'

'Was he having a relationship with your daughter, Mr Lambert?'

'You mean was he sleeping with her?'

'Exactly.'

Lambert shook his head and hoped they believed him. He wasn't being too convincing. He wouldn't have believed him.

'She had left Simon her husband, you know,' he said. 'No great loss. He was a waster, but I couldn't protect her.'

'She left him, didn't she?' the woman asked. 'She came back to live with you.'

Lambert nodded. The awful taste in his mouth made him scowl. It seemed they knew everything. 'I couldn't protect her,' he said. 'Do you understand what I'm saying. I couldn't protect her. She wouldn't listen.'

'Lately she lived here with you and her lover, didn't she?'

He kept nodding. No point in denying it. He pictured Laura in her bedroom, laughing with such carefree abandon, her head thrown back, hands on her stomach. His little girl, grown so big, grown so alien. The tears came again. The room dissolved totally.

'Your daughter lived here with Norma Illingworth, didn't she?' the woman was saying. 'They lived together as a couple.'

'Not very respectable really,' the male detective said. 'Being a lesbian. It isn't really fashionable in your kind of circles.'

'Did you know your daughter was a lesbian?'

Of course he had known. How could he not have known? She had taunted him with the fact. It wasn't right. It wasn't natural. It wasn't respectable. But then, she was his daughter. What could he do about it. Suffer in silence and pretend it wasn't happening. He looked blindly about the room but could see nothing.

'But she liked men too, didn't she Mr Lambert? There were other lovers. Norma didn't have her all to herself. Did that cause a bit of jealousy?'

Lambert was thinking fast, his face buried in his hands as he acted the grief-stricken parent. The police had got it totally wrong and didn't realize it. Perhaps he could turn that to his advantage. But he had to be careful. One word out of place and he would ruin the carefully mapped plan.

'Was one of those lovers called Robert, Mr Lambert?'

'I don't know.'

'Do you know where Norma Illingworth is?'

He didn't respond. He pretended to weep. It was a pretence, though the tears were real enough. He was a distraught father, in a state of shock after his bereavement. Surely they would have the sense to go away and leave him alone with his misery.

'Maybe it would be better if we came back tomorrow, Mr Lambert? Get yourself a good night's sleep.'

They were gone. When Lambert looked out between his fingers the room was empty. He used the heels of his hands to dry his eyes properly and drank what was left of the brandy.

He checked the window. The reporters were gone too. The street was much quieter, the shops had closed. Litter flapped about in a strengthening breeze, catching under the tyres of the parked cars. The Silk Cut ad transformed into a jar of coffee and then into a jet black motor car speeding into a blood-red sunset. A cat sat on the wooden walkway in front of the hoarding licking its paws. Its fur shone with a silver halo from the tungsten floodlights on either side of it. Its eyes blazed back into Lambert's.

He turned back into the room. He crossed it, walking unsteadily to the door that led back into his private office. It was a small square room with a table, chair, four filing cabinets, and a collection of professional certificates hanging on the wall. It confused him that there was no one in the room. He stood, swaying slightly, trying to concentrate on the riddle set up in front of him. How had he ever allowed all this to happen. The answer stepped out from behind the door.

'Norma,' he said, swallowing a mouthful of bitter tasting saliva. 'They've gone. You can come out now.'

# 43

*Friday, 19.59*

After Lambert, Fyfe and Moya decided to call it a day and go for a meal. They decided against a restaurant after reading a succession of menus posted outside. Instead Fyfe bought a Chinese carry-out banquet for two people: tomato egg flower soup, lemon chicken, pork with cashew nuts, char siu with beansprouts, fried rice. Moya went to the off licence next door to get a bottle of wine and then into the corner shop further along for a couple of tins of dog food and a packet of Good Boy biscuits.

'Careful we don't get these mixed up now,' she said as the tops were taken off the silver cartons while the chunks of dog meat were being spooned out on to plates for Jill and Number Five.

After Moya had dumped her stuff in the bedroom, they sat on the carpet in the living-room in front of the fire with the three-piece suite pulled in behind them to stop draughts. The curtains were drawn. The standard lamp shone down on their barricaded space, leaving the rest of the room in greyness. The selection of foods on the tray between them steamed copiously but before they had started the soup the two dogs had wolfed their stuff in the kitchen and come through. They jumped over the arm of the sofa and lay down on the higher level to watch the humans eat.

'Just like children,' Moya said. 'Afraid they might be missing something.'

'Aren't we all.'

'What do you make of old Daddy Lambert then? Poor old guy. It must be terrible to see your daughter die like that. The death's bad enough and then there's the scandal.'

'We might get more sense out of him when he's sober.'

'Once he's sober he may not want to talk about it. Remember he's the very essence of respectability.'

'He's a sad, lonely old man.'

'Standing by while his daughter's indulging in deviant sex in the room next to his.'

'His daughter. His own flesh and blood.'

'Maybe that's why Simon Wright got so angry when we asked for the names of Laura's lovers. It must be quite a blow to an ego like his to have his wife leave him for another woman.'

'It would certainly kick the feet from under me.'

'But she can't have been all queer, not if she was having a fling with Ron Gilchrist.'

'Variety is the spice of life.'

'Or death in this particular case.'

Moya opened the wine and they clicked tumblers. The food was hot and spicy. It didn't last long. The wine, too, went quickly. They discussed the case with their mouths full, sifting through the theories, always running up against the *non sequitur* of the love note from Bobby clutched in Laura's dead hand. Deliberately designed to mislead, or a crucial piece of evidence? Who the hell was this Bobby/Robert person.? The sheer clumsiness of the suicide scenario was strange, with Gilchrist so obviously a murder victim too. Simon Wright, about to benefit from a handy financial windfall, was the hot favourite. He looked as guilty as sin. Pity his name wasn't Robert. That would just about have clinched it.

Fyfe stretched out on the floor and balanced his head against a cushion on the chair. Moya stacked the empties on the tray and lifted it out of the way. Number Five stirred herself and went to investigate possible left-overs.

Moya copied Fyfe's resting position with her head against a

cushion on the opposite chair so that they were lying alongside each other, facing each other. The dogs watched them from the sofa.

'No more shop talk,' Moya said. 'We're off duty now until morning.'

'You're the boss,' Fyfe told her.

'Good.'

'That's the beauty of staying away from the office.'

'We can make our own rules.'

'I would say we've earned some time off over the last few days.'

'Some time to ourselves.'

'Besides we've lost the chance to beat Isotonic's crime-solving record.'

'So tell me something about yourself.'

'You first.'

'What do you want to know?'

'Did you really beat up Robert Ross after he had fooled you the last time?'

'Just a little bit. No bruising where it shows, that's the secret.'

'Did you really?'

'Of course not. He's a pathological liar.'

'And you've never told an untruth in your life?'

'Never.'

'I believe you. What other secrets have you got?'

Plenty, Fyfe thought, but he wasn't going to tell her about them. He didn't let her know that the floorboards under the carpet where she was lying so comfortably were saturated with the blood of the man he had shot through the window to stop him murdering his wife Sally. He didn't tell her about Angela and the money they had stolen, which was now hidden under his garden shed. He didn't tell her how, as a role model for the modern policeman, he was a non-starter. Instead he strung together a few inconsequential facts and didn't make himself sound very interesting at all.

When he had finished Moya had her turn. She went easy on the hard luck dimension of a loving mother left by a selfish father to bring up a child on her own. She decided she knew him well enough to complain that she believed her career was being held back by time-serving men who didn't like to see a mere woman rise above them.

Towards the end she suddenly realized that she should have been packing for her Paris weekend but Ian Dalglish hadn't bothered to try to contact her to say he was sorry after their last row. Well, she wasn't going to phone him. The portable was on the mantelpiece with Fyfe's car keys. It wouldn't require many detective skills to find her, but he hadn't even made the effort. Let the selfish swine enjoy his own company, she decided. That would teach him.

Maybe she should tell Fyfe more about her erratic love life, she thought. She could cry on his sympathetic shoulder. He would be understanding. There was obviously a mutual attraction between them. It seemed that he instinctively understood more than she had told him already. She liked him. She had felt herself growing closer to him throughout the day. It would be nice to kiss him as long as he didn't expect anything more as a matter of course. Friends could exchange kisses without guilt. Kisses and hugs. Won't you be my friend, David? she thought.

Moya closed her eyes and pretended to sleep. It gave Fyfe the chance to observe her closely, to look at her face and notice the miniature laughter lines and the tiny kink in her nose. As he had done all day from a distance, he admired the swelling of her chest below the white blouse tucked into the wide belt at her waist, and her bony wrists and long fingers, and the gentle curve of her thighs, and the lovely ankles crossed one on top of the other and sheathed in black.

She was smiling broadly. She must know he was looking at her. Why else would she be lying back and enjoying it so? He wondered what she would do if he called her bluff. If he leaned forward and kissed her on the lips. The urge was becoming compellingly strong. Maybe he was psychic? Maybe he really could read her mind and that was precisely what she wanted him to do? Maybe she was silently urging him on, only he was too stupid to realize it. He looked up at Jill for moral support. Jill looked doubtful. But then she was likely to be jealous so she wasn't the best of judges.

He should have shaved. A definite roughness had returned to his chin despite Sergio's special the previous morning. Fyfe got onto his knees and crawled over to be nearer Moya. She must be aware of him approaching her. His body had blocked off the heat from the fire. If she wanted him to stop all she had to do was open her eyes and warn him off. Yet she still lay there, eyes shut, still smiling. It was all set up. They wouldn't be interrupted. He had deliberately switched off the portable. If Moya had noticed he would have said it was an accident. What was he waiting for? A written invitation?

He hesitated. Never mind what Moya wanted. Did he want to do this? Did he want to get involved with another woman just when he and Sally seemed to be getting on so well together after all their troubles. Most of his problems stemmed from an inability to resist women. Why didn't he nip this particular problem in the bud. Save himself some grief. Besides, she had told him about her boyfriend back home. He looked over at Jill for guidance. She was no help. He was on his own.

# 44

*Friday, 20.15*

Matthewson finished entering his notes to the computer system. He was cutting it fine in getting to his rendezvous with Janet Dunbar but he would make it. He had told no-one about what she had said. She was his rabbit to be pulled out of the hat in front of everyone else at tomorrow morning's big case conference when everybody came together.

He grabbed his coat and was on his way to the stairs down to the rear car park when his phone rang. He went back to answer it.

'DS Matthewson, how can I help you?'

'The very man. This is Assistant Chief Constable George Rusling in Inverness, sergeant. I need to contact DI McBain immediately.'

Matthewson had reached across the desk to get the phone. He rested on his elbows, jarring himself so that his teeth

138

bit into his tongue and bounced off as if it was a piece of rubber.

'Yes sir,' he said. 'She is with DCI Fyfe. I have his mobile number here.'

'I have it too but the phone appears to be switched off or out of range. Do you know where they are.'

'Yes sir. They're still working on the inquiry. The phone may be off if they are interviewing somebody.'

'I need to speak to DI McBain urgently. Where is she spending the night. Can you give me the name of the hotel.'

Matthewson bit his tongue, regretting the act because it was already tender from the previous bite. Fyfe, wearing his black eye as a battle honour, had joked about taking Moya back to his flat to ply her with drink and seduce her. It was only a joke but Matthewson was quite clear there was some regulation or other that prevented them hiring out their private property to visiting officers. He couldn't clipe on his boss. He might need a return favour some day and it was more likely to come from Fyfe than from an assistant chief on another force. Loyalty ran deep, especially when promotion assessments were compiled. But this was an assistant chief constable asking and the inquiry was live. It had to be important.

'It's not a hotel, sir.'

'Guest house then.'

'I can't quite recall. DCI Fyfe will be at home later tonight. He'll be able to tell you.'

'No time for that. I need to know where he is now, sergeant.'

'I'm not exactly sure, sir.'

'I think you are, sergeant. Look if DI McBain was my escort I might want to get conveniently lost as well.'

'I don't know what you mean, sir.'

'Well you can't be that clever a detective.'

'Maybe they're walking the dogs?'

'What dogs? They're supposed to be on duty, aren't they? Look this is urgent, top priority. I need to know where Fyfe and McBain will be. It's to do with the murder inquiry.'

'I could probably get a message to him, sir.'

'If you can get a message to him you know where he is so I can deliver my own message. Tell me.'

Matthewson stopped stalling and told Rusling the address of the flat. What else could he do, he reasoned. It wasn't as if Fyfe was serious when he joked about seducing her. Surely they wouldn't actually be caught with their pants down? Surely not? He tried to phone Fyfe but clipped female vowels informed him the phone was switched off and he should try again later.

Matthewson shrugged helplessly and picked up his coat again. He could go round to the flat and warn Fyfe only he didn't know what he was supposed to be warning him about. Besides he had a date with a woman who was going to help him catch a murderer.

# 45

*Friday, 21.16*

Moya's mouth looked incredibly inviting. The tiny grooves on her lips, each one with its attendant shadow, drew Fyfe in. He was on one knee. One hand was on the chair, the other was on the floor so that she was encircled by his arms. He was sure her smile was growing wider as he lowered his head down towards her face. No going back now. He had made his decision. He closed his eyes.

He kissed her. Her forehead jerked forward and hit him on the bridge of the nose. Her hand slammed into his face. He fell to one side, collapsing over her legs and rolling off onto the carpet. She got up on her knees. Number Five was barking at the outbreak of excitement. Jill sat up on the sofa and looked down at him disdainfully.

'Are you all right?' she asked. 'What did you think you were doing? I got such a fright.'

Fyfe clutched his injured eye. The pain was intense. He could feel the skin growing larger under his hand, like a balloon inflating. Blood was leaking internally. He thought if he pressed hard enough he could keep it small. His nose was bleeding too. A warm sensation was spreading down his chin onto the front of his shirt. When he tried to speak he realized the blood was in the back of his throat and he choked on it. Moya knelt beside him with her arm round his shoulders.

'I'm sorry. I'm sorry,' she kept saying. 'You gave me such a fright, for goodness sake. I didn't mean to hurt you.'

Fyfe kept his head down. He was too embarrassed to look at Moya as she helped him to his feet and led him into the bathroom. Only cold water was available from the tap. What must she think of him and his clumsy efforts at seduction? His eye throbbed painfully like something attached to his head rather than something that was a part of it. What a bloody clown he was.

'It's my self-defence training,' Moya said. 'The instructor told me I had shit-hot reflexes. Oh dear, it looks as if your eye is swelling badly again.'

Fyfe looked in the mirror above the sink. The eye was closed, a smooth-edged slit in a rounded mound of black and blue. He held a handful of toilet paper to his nose to catch the blood. It rapidly turned pink. The blood that escaped spread sideways, caught up in the maze of stubble on his chin. At least Moya was laughing about it. Things couldn't be more colourful, but they could be worse. He wanted to apologize for his behaviour but was uncertain how to put it into words. God, he was embarrassed.

'I'd better go,' he said.

'Once the bleeding stops,' she insisted.

He did as he was told. He waited at the sink until the bleeding all but stopped and Moya stood behind him patting him on the back. The cold water seemed to make the blood clot more readily. After five minutes he was battered but no longer bleeding. His shirt and the lapels of his jacket were a mess. Moya dabbed at the blood with tissues and decided that she wanted to be more than friends. It was her nervous stupidity that had ruined what should have been a beautiful moment between them. If he didn't make another pass at her she would take the initiative.

'I'd better go,' Fyfe repeated. 'I'll leave you the dogs. They'll keep any ghosts at bay and I'll come back and get them in the morning.'

'That's very thoughtful of you.'

141

'Do you think so?'

'I'd better be going.'

'Why? I haven't had a chance to say sorry properly yet.'

Moya pushed him against the sink and kissed him on the lips, forcing his head back and running her tongue over his teeth.

'If you're going to kiss me, David, don't sneak up on me like that,' she said. 'Do it when my eyes are open. I prefer it that way.'

'Do you now,' Fyfe said, his confidence restored. 'I'm afraid I can only open one eye at the moment.'

'So I see. Never mind, the rest of you is in working order.'

She kissed him again, harder, making his head spin as the sensitive bruised flesh round his eye was stretched. This time he put his arms round her and pulled her in as tightly as he could. She felt as good as she tasted, staying in close as they paused for breath. He worried that the sink would not be able to support their combined weight and would come away from the wall.

'Careful,' he warned. 'The sink won't take this kind of punishment. You'll have us on the floor.'

'Do you believe in destiny, Chief Inspector?' Moya said breathily.

'Sometimes,' he replied, trying not to show how painful his eye was. 'Despite everything we've learned today.'

'A reason for everything.'

'A reason for us being alone together here.'

'What could that reason be? I haven't read it anywhere recently, have I?'

'Kiss me and you'll get a better idea,' she ordered.

He pulled her in and was just about to kiss her when the doorbell rang. It drilled into the silence between them, creating a physical barrier that prohibited further contact. Three times it stopped and three times it re-started, screaming its urgent message and destroying the mood of romance. The dogs were barking. Fyfe's nose started to bleed again.

'Who can that be?' Moya said angrily. 'It must be about the inquiry. I'd better answer it.'

She was gone before he could do anything about it. He turned and let the blood from his nose drip into the sink. He looked at his ravaged face in the mirror and sighed wearily.

'Destiny David,' he told himself bitterly. 'Looks like bloody destiny's got it in for you.'

# 46

*Friday, 21.32*

Moya couldn't believe it when she saw Ian Dalglish standing on the doorstep in front of her. There was an artificial smile on his face making him look like a grotesque parody of a Punch and Judy puppet. She was totally at a loss for words. The dogs behind her provided the excuse to turn round and avoid looking at him by pretending to calm them down. Her cheeks burned, twin red badges of embarrassment. Guilt at being caught in the act with Fyfe wrestled with anger at Dalglish for coming looking for her.

'What's the matter Moya,' Dalglish said. 'Surprised to see me?'

The mocking tone of his voice got through to her. Annoyance clashed with frustration. She stiffened. Anger got the upper hand. What was she? Some kind of schoolgirl caught in the act of two-timing her boyfriend? Well, yes, actually. Ignore the age element and that was a pretty fair description of the situation. Guilt calmed her down. She held Jill's head between her hands and wished her life could be as simple as an innocent dog's. She kissed Jill's cold nose.

'Aren't you going to invite me in then?' Dalglish said.

'What are you doing here, Ian?' She turned, hoping she would be able to stay in control. 'How did you find me?'

'You're hiding from me are you?'

'You know what I mean.'

'I've got friends in high places.'

'I'm working. Don't you realize I'm in the middle of running a murder inquiry.'

'From a private flat?'

'It's a convenient place to stay.'

143

'With Chief Inspector Fyfe by your side to see you through the night? It is his flat, isn't it?'

'So?'

'So maybe you're mixing a little business with pleasure.'

'Ian, how can you think such a thing? I'm a professional doing a job. We're working together on this inquiry. That's all there is to it. Nothing more.'

Dalglish relented a little, unsure of his ground. Moya watched his expression change from anger through uncertainty to regret. She could see that he didn't want to accuse her. His jealousy was overwhelming him. It appealed to her ego that he should be so upset. He had come all this way to find her. Thank God, it suddenly occurred to her, he had arrived in time.

How could she have considered cheating on him? How come she had ended up being seduced by Fyfe so soon after their first encounter when she had been convinced he was a typical cocky, patronizing male throwback? What was she playing at? David Fyfe was a threat, an amoral danger. Ian Dalglish was her future, her security. There was no contest. She would marry Dalgish now, just as soon as he asked her again. No messing around. That was settled in her mind.

It had been a narrow escape with Fyfe. Moya sighed deeply and shook her head at her impulsive foolishness. She shivered in the cold of the high-ceilinged hallway and stepped forward to kiss Dalglish on the cheek to begin the process of making-up.

'We're supposed to go to Paris tomorrow,' he said.

'I can't. Not now. Not until this inquiry is finished.'

'Don't worry, I understand. Edinburgh's a romantic city too.'

Dalglish came inside and embraced her fondly. Reasonableness had been restored, Moya thought gratefully. Her lustful aberration had been nipped in the bud. Another few minutes and she would have committed another crime of passion, one there was no legislation against. Now the embarrassment for her was that Fyfe was still in the bathroom bleeding into the sink. How was she going to get rid of him and retain her credibility.

Footsteps approached from behind. The dogs' claws scraped on the floor tiles as they moved back into the flat. The burning in Moya's cheeks was rekindled.

'You must be DCI Fyfe,' Dalglish said over Moya's shoulder. 'That's a colourful eye. You've been in the wars.'

'Goes with the job.'

Moya made the formal introductions. The two men shook hands and she looked from one to the other. Fyfe was holding a blood-stained tissue to his nose. The sense of absurdity made her light-headed and she covered her mouth to stop herself laughing.

'Nice flat you've got here,' Dalglish said.

'It's just sitting empty. We thought it would be a good idea to save the taxpayer some money on Moya's accommodation. Better than some grotty guest house.'

'Much better,' Dalglish agreed. 'Very cosy.'

'I'll see you in the morning, Moya,' Fyfe said. 'Bright and early. Don't stay up too late. Come on dogs. Time to go home.'

Moya closed the door behind him. It would be easy to explain the remnants of the Chinese meal as a working dinner she and Fyfe had shared. Nothing wrong with that. She hoped there was no other incriminating evidence lying around. They hadn't made it to the bedroom and started undressing. The sink was still firmly screwed to the wall, which was more than she had been, thank goodness. She was in the clear and her man was in a forgiving mood.

'You don't mind me staying the night, do you?' Dalglish asked.

'On the contrary, Ian,' going all dewy-eyed and girlish. 'I hate sleeping alone. You know that.' She pushed him ahead of her into the flat, grimacing at her self-conscious display of hypocrisy but perversely pleased that she was able to carry it off so convincingly.

# 47

*Friday, 22.00*

Matthewson saw the woman in the Philip Marlowe trench-coat pacing up and down beside the pair of phone boxes. Her hair was held back in a bushy pony tail held by a yellow scarf. The collar of the coat was pulled up round her face and the belt was loosely tied. One hand rested on a bag at waist level hung over her shoulder. She smoked intermittently, not inhaling but blowing the smoke upwards with unconscious film-star *élan*.

He had parked his car some distance away so that he could approach on foot by the bridge over the Water of Leith. She saw him and seemed to guess who he was straight away. She stopped pacing and waited for him at the window of the launderette. She threw down a cigarette butt and crushed it under her shoe. Black boots, Matthewson noted, with slightly elevated heels. Knee-length or thigh-length? He hoped desperately that she wasn't a time-waster. He needed something positive to give to Fyfe to make up for shopping him and the woman detective. God, what would happen if they were caught at it. Was it against regulations, like drinking on duty?

He crossed the road, past the round-faced clock on its stone pillar on the traffic island, and went up to her. There was hardly anyone else around except for a teenage boy in one of the phone boxes and occasional figures moving about in the distance.

'I'm Sergeant Matthewson,' he said, showing identification. 'Did you phone me?'

She nodded. 'Janet Dunbar.'

Close up, he could see her eyes were red with crying. She was an attractive woman, trying to look younger than she actually was. Her hair had light roots. Her face was just too heavily powdered. He felt sorry for her.

'What can you tell me, Janet?'

146

'I know Simon Wright. It's his wife that was found . . .'

'Yes, I know. What about Mr Wright.'

'He wants me to be his alibi.'

'What do you mean?'

'I was there last night, when you came. That's how I recognized you when you arrived.'

'Really.' Matthewson frowned, pretending he hadn't known.

'Yes. I hid in the kitchen and listened at the door.'

'Did you indeed? You and Mr Wright are friends?'

'You could say that.'

'Lovers?'

'I'm a married woman with two teenage children. We were having an affair. He was my bit on the side. That's why I'm here on this street corner. I couldn't ask you to come to my home.'

Matthewson held his hands up. 'I make no judgements, Janet,' he said. 'There but for the grace of God and all that.'

'I only seem to be able to make bad judgements. After you were gone, Simon asked me if I would give him an alibi.'

'And can you?'

'No. At first I thought it was a joke but he was waiting for me in the car park this morning. He threatened me.'

She began to fumble in her handbag for the cigarette packet. She extracted one and held it between her fingers, making no attempt to put it in her mouth. In her other hand she held a cheap gas lighter. A group of four people hurried past. Two drunks were arguing loudly on a corner one hundred yards away.

'How did he threaten you?' Matthewson asked.

'Well, he didn't threaten me exactly. It was his manner. He scared me. On Tuesday night I was supposed to meet him. It was our regular arrangement. We meet in a pub and go for a meal. I waited for hours but he didn't turn up. He came to my office on the Wednesday morning to apologize but he wouldn't tell me where he had been, just that it was business, emergency business.'

'He said that, did he?'

'Yes. And that was why I was at his house on Thursday. It was because we missed Tuesday. Then after you lot came he

147

asked me if I would be his alibi and I thought it was a bad joke until I read the papers today. They say that Laura Lambert was probably killed on Tuesday.'

She put the cigarette in her mouth and lit it from a shaky hand. Matthewson did not smile but he realized what was coming and composed himself to be ready for it.

'Simon must have murdered his wife on Tuesday night when he should have been with me.'

'Why do you think that?'

'I could smell her perfume on him, that's why.'

She sucked hard on the cigarette. The burning tobacco glowed fiercely. So Wright wasn't such a smart bastard after all, Matthewson was thinking. Now he had been caught lying they could really take him apart.

'Will you make a statement to that effect?' Matthewson asked.

'I'm a married woman. My husband doesn't suspect a thing.'

Matthewson didn't know how to answer her. He was elated. All he could think of was Wright's face when they confronted him with this information.

'I don't suppose there's any way to avoid my name being used?' she said.

'I'll try but it will be difficult, Janet.' He was lying. She would be the main witness. There was no way out for her. She couldn't remain anonymous. He said: 'If he killed his wife, you could be next.'

'Yes,' she agreed sadly, crushing the half-smoked cigarette underfoot. 'I'll give you your statement but not now. I need to go home to my family now before they suspect anything. Can you take me. It's not far.'

Matthewson took her elbow in the palm of his hand and guided her to the edge of the pavement. They waited patiently for a sudden convoy of four cars and a taxi to pass, then crossed the road. Matthewson had to consciously slow himself down to walk at her pace. He was excited. He had solved the murder mystery. Fyfe would be proud of him.

# 48

Douglas Lambert lay on the sofa the way the dead bodies were laid out in their coffins in the funeral parlour below him. He crossed his hands over his chest and felt the weak tremor caused by the regular beat of his old heart. Pat Gilchrist stood over him, looking down at him but right through him. She was talking to herself.

'It was Norma, the bitch. She killed Laura and then lured Ron up there on some pretext to set him up as the scapegoat. Everybody knew Ron was infatuated with Laura but he never touched her. Not once. I would have known. He didn't touch her.'

'Yes Pat, you're right.'

The tears were swelling behind Lambert's eyes but he resisted them. They were tears of self-pity anyway, not tears of genuine sorrow. He studied the light fitting. It was a simple copper-coloured, four-bulb affair hanging from a central stalk. One glass shade was cracked with a small fingernail-sized piece missing. The line of an ancient cobweb, like a thin trail of spittle, was strung between two others.

'They'll get her, wherever she is,' Pat said. 'I told them about her and Laura. How they were a couple. You knew too, didn't you Doug? You let them use the bedroom here. I don't know how you could do that.'

'She was my daughter.'

Pat grimaced horribly. Her whole face wrinkled up as if it was a rubber mask about to be peeled away. Lambert remembered Laura's face turning to him. Norma on her knees on the bed kissing her stomach. The triumph in their eyes. The insolence. The supremacy. The unnaturalness of it. The depravity.

'He was sleeping with her, Pat,' he said quietly.

149

'Who?'

'Your Ron. He was sleeping with her.'

'Nonsense. How do you know?'

'Laura told me.'

He was lying. Laura hadn't told him. Norma had. He could see that Pat was shattered by the information. She didn't argue because she had known all along and just didn't want to acknowledge the fact. Once he had brought it out in the open she could no longer avoid the truth. It affected her like an illness followed through by time-lapse photography. She visibly aged in front of him. Her skin became grey and settled flimsily around the bones beneath. All her illusions faded and died.

Only days ago he had planned to marry this woman and live with her for the rest of his life. Only last night he had slept with her, caressed her, comforted her, made asexual love to her. Now he couldn't care less. He felt nothing for her, absolutely nothing. They were strangers again and he wanted to hurt her so that he could gain some perverse consolation by not suffering alone.

He heard the door open and close, footsteps down the stairs, out into the street. Only once he was alone did Lambert begin to cry. He put his hands to his face and massaged the damp skin below his eyes.

# 49

*Friday, 22.41*

The car phone rang when Fyfe was ten minutes from home. He decided not to answer it. Twelve rings. A round dozen. Obviously nothing too important.

Fyfe tried not to think about Moya back at the flat with her jealous boyfriend. He wasn't sure how to take her final act of kissing him so passionately before kicking him out. Where did they stand now? Who was going to be more embarrassed when they met again to continue the murder inquiry? For Christ's sake, all he wanted was a warm body to cuddle in with. Never mind. At least he had Sally waiting to comfort him.

He occupied his mind by making up a good story to explain his injuries, a better story than standing like a statue while somebody crashed a chair over his head. My eye? It's nothing really. You should see the other bastard. The bloody nose? Well, I tried to get my leg over this sexy detective and she hit me with a right hook.

Fyfe hoped Sally would be asleep. He had warned her he might not be back until after midnight. She was almost certainly asleep by now. Fine by him. He would undress and climb in beside her. No explanations necessary for excited dogs, blood-stained shirts or black eyes if he stayed in the dark. He examined his unshaven battered face in the rearview mirror. He wasn't a pretty sight, but then he never had been.

The big Volvo turned off the road, fitting through the gateway with only inches to spare on either side. The lights were on downstairs in the house. That meant Sally was still up, reading a book or watching a late film on the television. He was even more surprised to see a strange car parked in his usual space in front of the garage. Visitors? At this time of night? A spasm of foreboding made his chest tighten. He should have answered the phone a few minutes ago. Something was wrong here.

He got out of the car and walked to the main door. It was unlocked. The dogs whimpered quietly behind him, anxious to greet Sally. He could hear low voices coming from the living-room. He quickened his pace along the hallway, pushed the door open, stepped inside. Sally was sitting on the arm of a chair. Her hair was hanging loose. When she looked across at him it hid her face. She was wearing a dressing-gown that had fallen open to show her legs. There was a man sitting in the chair. His balding head was pressed to her chest and one arm was over her waist with the hand resting lightly on her hip. Sally was holding his head. There was a lipstick mark on the scalp where she had kissed him.

'What the fuck,' Fyfe said.

The dogs started barking. A rush of inarticulate anger barnstormed through Fyfe's veins. The blood vessels in his nose burst and blood leaked into his mouth. He ran across the room.

151

Sally tried to stand up. The stranger tried to disentangle himself from her but didn't succeed before Fyfe had him by the jacket, dragging him to his feet. Sally was shoved unceremoniously to one side.

'It's not what you think,' said the man, holding his hands up in an attitude of surrender. 'Honestly, it's not what you think.'

He was relatively young. The lack of hair made him look older from a distance. His face was unlined. His nose was thin and straight. His fingernails professionally manicured. He had a thick gold chain round his neck.

'Dave. Stop it.' Sally tried to force herself between them. 'Will you listen for a moment.'

Jill and Number Five stood off, bouncing on their front paws and barking furiously. Fyfe pushed Sally away with one hand and swung his fist at the man. The punch looped through the empty air. Its momentum pulled Fyfe after it. He overbalanced and landed face down in the chair. When he scrambled round the man was where he had been with his hands stretched out in front to hold Fyfe at bay.

'Will you stop it,' Sally screamed, jumping on his back.

He dislodged her and lunged forward. The man easily moved out of reach. Number Five jumped at him snapping but he held her off. Jill went for his ankles but he danced out of reach. Fyfe growled like an animal and wiped blood from his nose with the back of his hand.

'I really don't want to hurt you,' the stranger said.

'I'll fucking hurt you then, you bastard.'

'Stay back.'

'Too late, pretty boy.'

'I'm warning you.'

Fyfe lunged with another punch and missed. He feinted another punch and at the last moment changed it to a shoulder charge. The man stepped aside but Fyfe caught hold of his arm as he went past and managed to stay close in. He gripped onto the sleeve and twisted to have a clear route of attack. This time the punch he threw was heading straight for its target until the man suddenly pirouetted ballet-style on one leg and brought his other leg flashing round in a graceful curve. Fyfe had a glimpse of the pattern of holes in a black brogue shoe before it connected with the right side of his forehead. He went down like a ton of bricks, unconscious before he hit the ground.

# 50

A shockwave of mental clarity hit Eddie Illingworth as he missed the step he was taking and the involuntary stamping of his foot jarred up through his body. He was on the central stairway of his tenement block, one landing below his flat. He recognized the peeling paint on the walls. He was hopelessly drunk and a woman was pulling him along by the hand. He had no idea who she was, where he had met her, or where he had been. The last thing he remembered was leaving the office after the unsettling visit by the two detectives doing their tap-dancing impersonation of Fred Astaire and Ginger Rogers. He had no conception of the time or the events that had elapsed since then.

His companion tugged at him but Illingworth stood firm. She turned to face him. The long overcoat swung like a cloak, disturbing the freezing air. Her breath was vaporizing as it came out of her mouth, making her head look as if it was about to burst into flames. Tightly curled dark hair, green eye shadow and huge spider lashes. One dangling ear-ring was lower than its neighbour. Her legs were too thick for the mini-skirt. She was a complete overweight stranger.

'Come on, lover boy,' she leered back at him. 'You're not getting cold feet after everything you promised me?'

It wasn't cold feet he had, but a sudden case of frostbite. What had he promised her? Who was she? He wished he had stayed blackout drunk until the inevitable was over. Then his penance would have been merely the embarrassment of waking up and getting rid of her in the morning. This was like waking up in the middle of a painful operation with the first cut about to be made in his tender flesh. Whatever he had promised her it had not been stimulating conversation.

There was no point in resisting. She led him up the next flight of stairs as easily as a mother pulling a reluctant child. Her backside moved solidly under the thick material of her coat. She balanced expertly on long stiletto heels. Outside his door she pushed him to the front, put her chin on his shoulder and slipped her hands into both his trouser pockets.

'Is this a bunch of keys in your pocket or are you just pleased to see me?'

Illingworth flinched as his genitals were squeezed none too gently. He didn't like to object too forcibly. Intuition warned him that she was the type of woman who would enjoy inflicting pain much more if she realized it wasn't being properly appreciated. Her teeth were on his neck. They felt worryingly sharp. He felt alarmingly fragile but at the same time was beginning to think that this might not be too bad after all.

He unlocked the door and they tumbled inside, almost falling over each other but being saved by the walls of the narrow hallway. He went straight for the kitchen where he kept his household supply of booze. A few drinks more would tip the scales back into the blackout. His pick-up still had her hands in his pockets. She was towed after him. Before he had the chance to reach for the cupboard she had spun him round and forced him back against the cork noticeboard hanging on the wall. She kissed him, bouncing his head off the wall. Her mouth covered not only his lips but his nose as well so that he couldn't breathe. Her pelvis ground hard into him. He struggled to break free but she was a strong woman. The holiday postcards pinned to the board were knocked off. Then the gas and electricity bills and all the other accumulated debris of notes and reminders. While they were still fluttering to the floor she stopped trying to suck his face off and stood back. He breathed in thankfully.

'That's just for starters, lover boy,' she said hoarsely, wiping away a smear of stray lipstick. 'Where's the bedroom?'

Illingworth pointed to the door beyond the kitchen. The whole noticeboard crashed down behind him among the litter

154

at his ankles. She made an obscene gesture with her tongue and flounced out.

He went for the booze cupboard, aware that he would need all the help he could get to survive the coming encounter. But before he could get hold of a bottle he was transfixed by a high-pitched scream that sliced through him like a buzz-saw. He reacted slowly, pulled towards the sound. He stepped outside the kitchen door just as the woman came running out of the bedroom. The look of unquenchable lust in her eyes had changed to one of absolute terror. She shoulder-charged Illingworth, knocking him to the ground and winding him. She ran over the top of him. One sharp heel stabbed into the little finger of his left hand, ripping it open. Then she was gone out of the front door, her screaming trailing behind her, fading gradually, as though she had jumped over a sheer precipice and was sky-diving earthwards.

In the corridor, Illingworth picked himself up and looked from bedroom to front door, undecided which to go to first. 'Was it something I said?' he asked the empty flat.

The screaming stopped with the ground-floor door thumping shut. Illingworth frowned. Drunkenness made him sway on his feet and think in disconnected sequences that failed to make any sense of what had happened. He looked at his bleeding finger but didn't feel any pain. He held it in his good hand to stem the blood-flow and decided the bedroom would offer the best explanation of what the fuss was about.

He saw Norma's body from the doorway. It was lying diagonally across the floor, face down on the rectangle of light blue scatter carpet. He must have realized it was his sister Norma immediately but it took several seconds for his brain to acknowledge the fact. She had one arm stretched out in front of her. It pointed to the antique hourglass, showing that a small section of the wooden framework had been snapped. The top bulb was broken, cracked like an eggshell. A hole had been punched in it and the jagged edges of the break were dripping with a green viscous fluid. Some of the sand inside was stained green. The inside of the curving glass was smeared with it, like moss on a wall. On the floor he noticed an empty plastic bottle

155

of supermarket shampoo and an old flat iron he used as a door stop.

Illingworth moved into the room and stood over his sister. By shifting his position he saw her from a different angle. On the carpet he saw the cartoon fishes nibbling at her. He remembered Thursday morning and her trance, her painful glimpse of the future. When he had heard about Laura and the discovery of her body at the loch he had been suitably impressed, disconcerted and terrified by her psychic ability. But he had been wrong. It had been a prophetic vision of Norma's own death. Here was the proof lying at his feet. Blood dripped from his finger onto her.

He stared down helplessly, hoping a vision would come to him to tell him what to do. Poor Norma wasn't dead. He could see she was still breathing. She had always hated his hourglass. She said it had a bad aura, had seen too many bad things in the past, had recorded too many deaths and not enough births. He had laughed at her. Once before she had tried to break it. Soon after he moved in, she had arrived back one night stoned out of her mind and tried to shove it out the window. He had taken it off her and tried to quieten her. 'Some day I'll have to stop it,' she told him as he held her down in her bed. In the morning she remembered nothing.

The shampoo inside the hourglass was coagulating in the fine sand, thickening it, blocking the filament aperture. As Illingworth watched the sand was prevented from running freely. The thin stream was choked off. Time stood still.

## 51

*Friday, 23.05*

Moya had been won over. All the anger was gone. She was glad that Ian Dalglish had taken the time and trouble to seek her out and stop her from doing something that she would have hugely regretted come the morning. It was good to think he could be so jealous and so desperate as to enlist the help of an off-duty assistant chief constable. And so they had kissed, made up, and made love in front of the fire with the debris from the Chinese meal she had eaten with Fyfe still stacked up on the tray beside them. She luxuriated in the afterglow of satisfying sex. Paris was postponed by mutual consent until the next weekend she had free.

Dalglish was asleep beside her, bundled under the covers they had dragged through from the bedroom. She stroked his forehead and counted her blessings. A career was important but it didn't keep you warm in bed at night. It didn't get jealous because it loved you madly. It didn't travel the length of the country to find you. Dalglish hadn't got round to asking her to marry him. They hadn't had much time to talk. But she knew he would eventually. The quicker the better, as far as she was concerned now. She had learned a lot from the near miss with Fyfe. More than he would ever know, and among it all he had taught her there was more to life than being the world's greatest detective. She was grateful to him for that.

The ringing of the doorbell interrupted her placid thoughts. Reality crowded in. The murder inquiry she was supposedly in charge of was still in progress and she had not been in touch for several hours. Anything could have happened. That would be Fyfe at the door, back to tell her how they had found the killer and closed the file while she was otherwise occupied putting her love life back on an even keel. The bastard now had the perfect opportunity to patronize her and put her down. She had no alternative but to grin and bear it. She could hardly believe she had acted so recklessly such a short time before. It must have been a kind of temporary insanity. At least now she was back living and loving in the real world.

Moya got dressed as quickly as she could. Dalglish tossed and muttered but didn't wake up. By the time she went to answer the door the bell had only rung twice. Fyfe showing consideration, she speculated. Before she opened the door she paused and took a deep breath. She wasn't going to be the one to suffer agonies of embarrassment. She was going to stare him out, force him to look away first. She would slap his face if he dared to try and intimidate her. The fact that it was Bill

Matthewson on the doorstep confused her. When she tried to speak she couldn't get the words out. It was getting to be a habit, this opening of doors to find someone unexpected on the other side.

'Is DCI Fyfe with you, Ma'am?' Matthewson asked. 'I've got some important news.'

'No,' Moya replied, composing herself. 'He's not here.'

'It's just that I thought he might be.'

'He's not.'

'Do you know where he is?'

'Not exactly.'

Behind her Moya could hear Dalglish shuffling along the corridor. She saw that Matthewson was pushing his tongue into his cheek to prevent himself laughing. She turned and saw Dalglish with a blanket round his waist and over his shoulder. There was a massive purply-red love bite on the right-side pectoral muscle down from his shoulder. She always did that to him on the good nights.

'Who is it, darling?' Dalglish asked sleepily.

'Police business, Ian. Go back inside. It's cold out here.'

She pulled the interior door closed and turned back to Matthewson. He was standing with his hands behind his back trying not to look amused. She didn't attempt to explain who Dalglish was. Moya struggled not to smile as well. Her reputation would be torn to shreds by the boys in the locker-room. Still, she reasoned, she had joined them not beaten them and it was better to be regarded as a sexy item rather than a frigid one.

'What do you want DCI Fyfe for?'

'I've got new evidence in the murder and he's not answering his phone.'

'He makes a habit of that, doesn't he? Why don't you tell me?'

'I usually work with Mr Fyfe.'

'I appreciate your loyalty but he's working with me on this one. I'm in charge of the case and you can tell me.'

'Yes Ma'am.'

Matthewson told her Janet Dunbar's story about the broken date and the threats over the alibi from Simon Wright. Moya didn't let herself show any outward emotion but she got steadily more excited listening to the details. It looked as if they had something definite on him. A little more judiciously applied pressure and he might crack wide open. By the time Fyfe deigned to reappear the case would be closed. That would put him in his place rather nicely.

'Wright came in voluntarily for his interview yesterday,' Matthewson said. 'If we lift him now we've got six hours to play with before we have to charge him. I reckon he won't last.'

Moya thought about it and liked the idea. 'Let's do it. I'll be with you in a few minutes and we can go shake him awake.'

She went back into the flat to explain to Dalglish that he would have to sleep the rest of the night alone. He would understand.

## 52

*Friday, 23.24*

'How are you feeling, darling? You've been in the wars, haven't you? Head sore?'

Fyfe blinked and saw Sally's face very close to his. It seemed distorted, out of proportion as though he was viewing it through one of those spyholes drilled in doors.

'My jealous lover,' she crooned. 'What did you think you were playing at? You've nothing to worry about.'

Her face resolved itself into focus. She had the same kind of enigmatic smile that Moya had worn in the flat before reversing him up against the sink in the bathroom. Was this some kind of conspiracy?

'It's very flattering to have men fight over me. Not very civilized though.'

The memory of the black brogue and the bald-headed ballet dancer came surging back to him. And then there was Sally sitting on this guy's knee kissing him. Adultery in action.

159

'I've run a bath for you,' Sally said. 'You know how you like a nice hot bath. This one is roasting hot.'

The adrenalin rush, fuelled by the sight of Sally with another man so soon after the frustration of being kicked out by Moya, had been like a massive shove in the back. Here was somebody he could take it out on. Only it hadn't turned out like that. Fyfe moved his head and his brain seemed to rattle inside his skull, causing a painful fireworks display of coloured lights to explode across his field of vision.

'Take it easy darling. Careful now. Come with me.'

Fyfe moved slowly and obediently, allowing himself to be led by Sally. The headache gradually subsided to be replaced by a sensation that his head was twice the size it should have been. Sally took him upstairs and into the bathroom.

'There now. Take your clothes off. I'll get you something to help you relax.'

He did as he was told. The wall mirror was misted over with steam from the bath. He wiped it clear and saw that there was now bad bruising around both eyes, extending right across his face like a visor. A pair of pink bloodshot eyes were deeply inset in the puffy flesh. A moustache of blood was crusted on his upper lip.

He stepped into the bath and the shock of the heat made him gasp, but it cleared his head. The room became abruptly brighter. He lowered himself into the water until he was submerged up to the neck and his whole body tingled. He kept going until he was completely under the water and the tingling was particularly fierce on the bruised bits of his face. When he came up for air Sally was sitting on the side of the bath, offering him a glass of whisky.

'Who was he then?' Fyfe asked.

'Oliver. He is a student in my department at the university.'

'What was he doing here?'

'I'm his staff-appointed counsellor. He had a personal crisis.'

'At this hour. Your crisis or his?'

'His.'

'Confessing he was madly in love with you, was he?'

'Not quite.'

'Then why were you cuddling the bastard. I thought . . .'

160

'It was obvious what you thought.'

'Well then. What was going on?'

'Oliver came to me to make a confession. It took a lot of doing.'

'What?'

'He came to confess that he was gay. He didn't know who else to talk to. I was comforting him.'

'Gay? But . . .'

'They're not all limp-wristed nancy boys, you know.'

'What is he then? Some kind of karate expert?'

'Tae Kwon-Do actually. Brown belt I understand.'

'Just my luck.'

Fyfe felt like an utter idiot for the second time in the space of a few hours. He sipped his whisky and ducked below the water again for as long as he could hold his breath. His head deflated gradually to more normal size. When he came up for air Sally was still sitting there on the edge of the bath. Her dressing gown had fallen open to show her legs. He realized she was assuming that all his injuries, bloody nose, included, had been inflicted by her gayboy pal. That saved him from having to bother with a false explanation. Neither would he volunteer to tell Sally about the law of prophecy that had been dinned into him lately and had just proved itself accurate once more; the most obvious explanation is likely to be the wrong one.

'What are you?' Fyfe asked. 'Some kind of nursemaid?'

'I'm a shoulder to cry on. He's just a young lad. His parents have disowned him.'

'So you're the mother substitute.'

'And you're the red-eyed bull at the gate to remind him of the hostile world outside.'

'Is he gone?'

'What do you think? He made quite a mess of you, didn't he? You gave him no option. You backed him into a corner and went down fighting. My loyal white knight in shining armour. He passes on his apologies.'

'Very considerate of him. How long was I out for?'

'Not long. It's nice to know you're prepared to fight for me.'

'Even if I lose.'

'It's the thought that counts. How's the head.'

'Still attached to my shoulders.'

'Do you think I should get a doctor?'

'It's only my head. Nothing vital.'

'Hurry up and come to bed. I'll mop your fevered brow for you.'

That curious smile again, the female equivalent of a sporting handshake with the loser at the end of a particularly one-sided contest. She leaned over the bath, one hand on his knee to balance herself. He screwed his eyes shut and braced himself. She kissed him delicately on the tip of the nose.

'Sorry Sally,' he said.

'It's okay. Oliver saw the funny side of it.'

'I'm glad I didn't damage his sense of humour.'

'I hope he hasn't damaged yours. How's your double murder going?'

'It's going.'

'You must have had a busy day?'

'A pretty boring one. Knocked back at every turn.'

Fyfe admired his own suggestive wit. It was so impressive. Practice had made perfect. To round off the performance he wondered if he should pull Sally into the bath beside him, like it would happen in a romantic comedy film. They would make love and slop water all over the floor. It was good to be connected to her. Life had been a disaster when they were apart and he had been so lucky to get her back. He was a fool to risk losing her again by lying to her and attempting to play around with Moya. But that was his nature. He was a fool.

The handset hidden in Fyfe's jacket pocket on the bathroom floor began to ring. They both looked down at it.

'Will we answer it?' Sally asked. 'Or will we just go to bed.'

'If they're phoning at this time it must be important,' Fyfe said.

'Let's go to bed then,' she said but she didn't mean it.

Sally never argued when it was police business. She picked up the handset and handed it to Fyfe. He sat up to take it, careful not to cause the bath to overflow.

'DCI Fyfe here,' he said, adopting his formal telephone manner.

There was the sound of weeping and spluttering at the other

end of the line. And Fyfe's name repeated over and over again among unintelligible sentences. Finally a phrase established itself over the verbal static and it electrified Fyfe. He sat bolt upright and a wave splashed over the rim of the bath. Sally dodged out of its way, cursing, but Fyfe wasn't paying any attention to her. He was focused on the barely audible words coming over the phone.

'Bobby's dead. Bobby's dead.'

## 53

*Saturday, 00.37*

Moya almost yawned. She stifled it at the last moment, keeping her hands down so as not to draw attention to her contorting facial muscles. She just managed to stop it and no more. Matthewson stood behind her waiting patiently for the interrogation to start.

Here she was about to turn in a positive result on her first murder inquiry and all she could think of was how good it would be to close her eyes and go to sleep. It had been a long day, with hardly any time for rest in between waking up with Number Five in her bed, to making a pass at Fyfe, to finding physical consolation with Ian Dalglish. There had even been time for some detective work in between. Not hers, but she could make up for that now and take advantage of other people's efforts. That was the privilege of rank. All she had to do was fight off exhaustion and stay awake, of course.

Across the table from her sat Simon Wright. She hoped she didn't look as bad as he did. He had come quietly when they went to get him. It was almost as if he was waiting for them. He had not been drinking, there was no smell of alcohol on his breath, but he was definitely on something. It had been obvious from the moment they confronted him at his house. He seemed to be floating inside his own air-conditioned bubble, looking down on the world from a position of supreme unconcern. Now he sat opposite her with an annoyingly contented expression, swaying imperceptibly on his chair, watching his hands in his lap. He was in a dope-smoker's dwam. If they had searched his house they would probably have found a stash of cannabis or something harder like cocaine. That would have given them the excuse to hold him for longer than six hours. Too late now. If needs must, they could always run him home and turn him over again.

'Why did you lie to us, Simon?' she asked.

He lifted his head slowly and a languid grin spread over his face. Moya was able to see why women were attracted to him. With his defences down and the skin of villainy stripped away, he was boyishly handsome in a vulnerable goofy sort of way that made you want to hold him and squeeze him. She dug the heel of her right shoe into the top of her left foot. For goodness sake Moya, she told herself, will you get a grip on your hormones. She still could not believe what she had tried to do with Fyfe against the sink. Maybe shock was setting in like it did with accident survivors a few hours after the traumatic event when they realize what a narrow escape they have just had.

'First names is it?' he said. 'That's nice.'

'Come on, Simon, you know the score. You've been here before.'

'Earlier today, wasn't it? Or was it a previous lifetime?'

'I thought you didn't believe in that kind of stuff?'

'Doesn't matter if I believe or not, not if it's true.'

'New information has come into our possession since we last met.'

'Has it?'

'Yes. It indicates that you deliberately lied to us.'

'Does it?'

'Correct me if I am wrong, Simon, but did you not tell me that you intended to be entirely honest. You said you were telling us the truth, the whole truth, and nothing but the truth.'

Wright's grin widened. He put his elbows on the table and leaned towards Moya. He crooked a finger to call her closer but she stayed where she was. Matthewson moved a step nearer.

164

The tape recorder was running. Wright had once more confidently waived his right to have a lawyer present.

'I lied,' Wright said, finishing the statement with a splutter of emphatic laughter.

'You didn't tell the truth.'

'I lied.'

'Why did you lie, Simon?'

He sat back, still grinning. One arm was on the back of the chair. A finger drew circles on the table-top. 'In my experience when the police start cosying up using first names with suspects they usually turn out to have some solid evidence that they are about to deliver like a sucker punch to the jaw.'

'Perhaps we do,' Moya agreed.

'Go on then.' He stuck out his chin. 'Hit me with it.'

'You said you spent most of Tuesday evening with Janet Dunbar. She says in a sworn statement that you didn't.'

Wright rubbed his chin. 'Ouch,' he said, beginning to shadow box. 'The knock-out blow but he's up and fighting again. A right, a left, a feint to the body and an uppercut rocks his opponent.'

'Quit the play-acting Simon,' she snapped. 'Tell me the truth this time. No more mucking about.'

'Okay then, I'll come clean but it won't do you any good.'

'Why not?'

'This statement will be inadmissible in court because I am under the influence of drugs. A few pills, inhalation of the smoke from a burning substance that I wasn't quite sure about but can now recommend. With everything taken into account I'm out of my box.'

'Tell me anyway, Simon.'

'All right then. On Tuesday night I received a call which demanded immediate attention. I couldn't ignore it.'

'Why not?'

'Business before pleasure.'

'Who called you?'

'A friend.'

'A lady friend?'

He grinned slyly. 'Maybe. Definitely an old friend.'

165

'What did this friend want?'

'To speak to me.'

'What about?'

'To check.'

'To check what?'

'To check that everything was in place as we had planned.'

'And was it?'

'Oh yes.'

'What was the plan?'

'Patience, my lovely Inspector. I'll tell you. You'll work it out for yourself sooner or later anyway. You see, my old friend was leading me on and screwing me up. The whole plan has fallen apart now. Look at me. I'm a broken man.'

He spread his arms as wide as they would go and hiccuped violently. For a moment Moya thought he was going to vomit across the table into her lap but his head snapped back erect and his whole body suddenly went rigid.

'So who is this old friend then?'

He relaxed. His neck went down into his shoulders. His arms were lowered slowly, fingers rippling to imitate fluttering wings. The grin spread again.

'My old friend Bobby,' he said.

# 54

*Saturday, 00.42*

The Victorian towers and spires of Edinburgh Royal Infirmary pierced the sky like some Gothic house of horror. A light fog draped itself round the walls and windows of the sprawling hospital complex. The street-lights on Lauriston Place had beautiful multi-coloured haloes. Beneath them faceless people moved to and fro. Drunks staggered and sang. Couples clung together and walked in step through an erratic drizzle of rain. In the distance, the sound of a motor bike with a broken silencer seemed to make the air vibrate.

Fyfe parked his car opposite the gates that led to the casualty department. Jill replaced him in the driver's seat and watched him go down the slope. He had driven in to the hospital as fast as he could after the phone call from Illingworth. It had ended with a policewoman taking the phone from him and explaining the situation: Norma, close to death from an overdose, and little brother Eddie acting erratically and illogically after returning from a heavy drinking bout to find her lying on the floor. The incident was reported by neighbours who heard screaming and saw a woman running away from the flat. Eddie's pick-up apparently. He was found sitting cross-legged beside his sister thinking she was dead. But they found a faint pulse and rushed her to casualty. They knew about the warrant for Norma. Should she contact anyone else? No, Fyfe replied. He would organize all that and meet them at the hospital.

Fyfe's hair was still damp as he went through the heavy, scuffed-plastic swing-doors. He had not yet told anyone else. The car phone had rung once as he approached the outskirts of the city but he had ignored it. He briefly considered going to the flat to rouse Moya and let her in on the hunt for Bobby, their missing link. But in the end he didn't because he couldn't face the emotional hassle.

The waiting-area was strewn with bodies and old magazines. A group of six men drank coffee from the machine and conversed in conspiratorial whispers. A tattooed skinhead lay across three chairs snoring noisily. Two teenage girls, as thin as the cigarettes in their mouths, sat under a No Smoking sign and quietly wept for the evening's latest victim. A middle-aged woman with a small child holding the hem of her coat argued with a nurse behind the wire mesh security screen at the reception desk. Illingworth was in a corner, chairs gathered round him like a defensive wall. The policewoman was holding his hand, talking to him soothingly. She was tall and wide-shouldered with a pleasant round face. He knew her as Sandra but couldn't recall her second name. She saw him approach and stood up. He felt obliged to say the bruising round his eyes was the result of an accident and didn't matter although it was throbbing painfully. Illingworth stayed where he was, looking up but showing no signs of recognition.

'The woman's out of danger, sir,' Sandra said.

'And how's her little brother?'

'Not making much sense, I'm afraid. I don't know if he's in shock or just plain pissed out of his head. He smells like a brewery. He had your card, and I knew about the murder inquiry and all that, so I phoned you and put him on.'

'That was good thinking.'

'So was it the woman, then, sir? It was an overdose. Guilt got to her?'

'Looks that way doesn't it, Sandra. Take a break while I have a chat with our pal here. Give us five minutes and see if you can contact DS Matthewson or DI McBain and get them over here.'

Sandra moved out of the picture and Fyfe sat down beside Illingworth. Recognition had dawned but he still wasn't making any sense. Fyfe listened carefully as he muttered something about boatmen on lochs and distant islands but then he rambled on to the subject of girls on swings. He was reminiscing about his childhood. His breath smelled rotten.

'Had a good night Eddie?' Fyfe said. 'Bit of a nasty surprise at the end of it.'

Halfway through the sentence he realized he could be talking about himself in another context. Illingworth looked at Fyfe as if seeing him for the first time. 'I love her. We were very close, you know,' he said, crossing index and forefingers on both hands. 'We were like that, me and Norma.'

'She's going to be fine.'

'No she's not. She's going to die.'

'The doctors say she's out of danger.'

'What do doctors know? She knows she's going to die. She told me.'

Fyfe didn't argue. Somebody from the group of six kicked the coffee machine when it failed to deliver a cup down its stainless steel chute. They all turned their backs as the coffee dribbled out uselessly and a pair of uniformed security guards strolled past. They turned back to abuse the machine as a pair of differently uniformed nurses followed the guards. The woman at the reception desk ended her one-sided dialogue and sat down. The child climbed into her lap and started sucking its thumb.

'Why did you call her Bobby?' Fyfe asked.

'Why? I never did. She hated me using that name.'

'You used it to me over the phone.'

'Did I?'

'It's a nickname, is it? A private nickname?'

'Yeah. She got it at school. Her favourite teacher called her Bobby and it stuck. Miss Ralston always treated her like the teacher's pet. She died in a hill-walking accident when we were in fourth year. Norma's never let anyone call her it since then.'

Fyfe didn't flinch as a blast of beery breath caught him full in the face. Illingworth described Miss Ralston's death in detail. She was leading a school party up Ben Ledi when a bouncing rock caught her on the side of the head. A one in a million chance. The children carried her body down.

'Was there a reason?' Fyfe asked.

'For the death?'

'For the name? Why Bobby?'

'What do you call an old shilling? A bob.'

'How does . . .'

'Illingworth. Shillingworth. Bob. Bobby.'

'Obvious really,' Fyfe agreed. 'Once you know.'

# 55

*Saturday, 00.45*

Wright was talking spontaneously now. Moya didn't need to prompt him at all after establishing Bobby's real identity and experiencing a deep sense of satisfaction that they were now making significant headway. A large measure of that satisfaction was in doing it without Fyfe's help.

There was an interruption, a knock at the door. Moya impatiently waved away the offer of a message from Fyfe. Let him wait, she thought angrily, wherever he is. I don't need his help to get to the truth here. I'm in charge.

'Me and my old friend Bobby, sorry Norma, weren't an item, you understand,' Wright was saying. 'She didn't like men at all. Well, not much. I slept with her once. I don't know why. It seemed like a good idea at the time. It was how we went into business together but I called her Bobby because it really annoyed her. I don't know why. She wouldn't tell me. I can be a bad bastard like that. Ultimately though ours was purely a business relationship and it would have been good business too if it had worked as we planned. We were going to bump her off and collect the insurance money but we were biding our time. In the end it was too hurried. We fucked it basically.'

He stared up at the ceiling, momentarily lost in a private dream world. Then he looked across at Moya and the dumb smile returned. He scratched the top of his head to imitate the comedian Stan Laurel.

'Another fine mess they got me into too,' he said. 'Both of them. Janet rats on me in this life and Laura dumps on me from beyond the grave. Women. Can't live with them, can't live without them.'

'You were telling me about Norma and Tuesday night.'

'Sure. Bobby phones me, all excitable and panicky. "Laura's dead," she says. "What are we going to do?" She answered her own question. We would do as we had planned, complete with convenient scapegoat and the crazy magazine columns that Bobby had been planting over the months to point you police folk in the desired direction. The only difference was that we weren't talking about it any longer, we were in the middle of doing it and it needed doing quickly because she was already dead. Too quickly as it turned out. Too many mistakes, not enough composure. I was to brass neck the insurance, make a virtue of it, because you would inevitably find out anyway. I'm a lawyer. I know these things. We had it all planned but things just moved too fast for me. I lost control. I shouldn't have hassled poor Janet. I should have left her alone. But I couldn't. It's the difference between theory and practice. You can't plan for it. I never trusted Norma anyway. I always thought she had her own death wish. I should have known she would let me down.'

Wright laughed weakly. His stupid grin was fading into something more like a frightened scowl. He put his hands back into his lap and watched them carefully. Moya could see he was fraying at the edges, about to hit the drug-induced wall he was headed straight towards. He hiccuped, stiffened and looked round the room as though seeing it for the first time.

'This scapegoat? Was it Ron Gilchrist?' Moya asked.

'Who else? Good old Ron. Randy Ron. Dirty old man that he was. Laura sucked him in and blew him out in bubbles with Norma's encouragement. They toyed with him, took him up north to the cottage for clandestine visits. Teased him unmercifully.

Laura thought it was all being done so they could blackmail him. She was game for that. You know, pour a few drinks down his throat and get him in a compromising position, then threaten to go to his wife with the pictures. She didn't realise me and Norma were doing it to make him ripe for the part of jealous lover. The plan was Norma's brainchild, by the way. Circles within circles eh? Old guy with a bad heart. A decent shag would probably have killed him. Instead somebody else did. He didn't have the option of dying with a smile on his face. It's a funny old world, isn't it?'

He laughed again and hiccuped. His face was chalk-white. He retched silently, swallowing air, his entire body convulsing for a few moments before settling back into the chair.

'So you didn't kill him?'

Wright feigned surprise. He shook his head primly.

'Is it such a stupid question?' Moya asked, determined to stay in control of the interview. 'Either you or Norma surely?'

He kept shaking his head.

'Norma kills Laura and you help string good old Ron up? Do I have that right?'

Wright held his head in his hands and shook it forcefully. A scatter of braying laughs sprayed out from between his fingers. 'No, no Inspector. You haven't got it right at all. Norma, my old friend Bobby, didn't kill anyone. Norma came to see me on

171

Tuesday night. She was all flustered and anxious. She said Laura was dead and I should now help her take the body up to the loch like we had planned.'

'And what did you do?'

'I bottled it. I told her to leave me alone. It was nothing to do with me.'

'Not very gallant.'

'Smart though. Norma's a nutter. I should never have listened to her. I think back and I don't understand how we managed to even consider her daft plan.'

'So what did she do when you failed to live up to expectations?'

'Do? I didn't do anything. She fixed me with this stare that would have curdled milk and then she went away.'

'You expect me to believe that?'

'It doesn't matter if you believe it or not, not if it's true.'

'And what did you do?'

'I went home and put a pillow over my head. I tried to pretend none of it was happening.'

'So Norma's the killer, is she?'

'No. That was why we fucked up. Haven't you been listening to me? We weren't in control.'

Moya frowned. She thought she had followed the plot perfectly. She was annoyed with herself for missing some vital thread of the argument.

'Then who?' she asked, realizing that she sounded pathetic and indecisive and feminine and wishing she didn't.

Wright belched. The grin had been restored but now it contained a sinister edge. The eyes were glazed and totally vacant. Moya watched helplessly as he hit the wall. His head slumped down onto the table, bouncing a little like a hard ball. Matthewson reached over and shook him roughly by the shoulder but there was no response.

# 56

The room contained a bed, a saline drip, a bulky electronic heart monitor with a tiny screen, and a locker on wheels. The monitor screen glowed in the dim grey light. A lamp on top of the locker had its bright white light directed down and away to pool uselessly in a corner. There was a jug of orange juice too with a glass covered over by a skin of clingfilm to keep the dust out. Norma lay on the bed wrapped tightly in the white open-weave blankets. One tube went up her nose, another into her wrist. Wires from the monitor went under the covers to her chest. A nurse stood by her with two fingers on the pulse in her neck, checking it against the watch on her lapel. It seemed right to speak in whispers.

'I'm told she's out of danger,' Fyfe said.

'In a manner of speaking,' the doctor replied.

'How do you mean?'

'It's true to say she's out of immediate danger but in the longer term I would have my doubts.'

The doctor held out his hand and waggled it from side to side. Then he turned it into a fist and gave the thumbs down signal. He was a youngster with a baby face and a shirt collar at least two sizes too big for him. His white coat was grubby and the left hand pocket was missing completely. His name badge said he was Ken McInnes. The poor light made the downy hair on his upper lip glow strangely. He looked impossibly young, like a boy playing the part of a doctor in a school play. Fyfe rubbed his stubbly chin and just managed to stop himself fingertip-touching the bruising round his eyes.

'Tell me the worst that will happen?'

McInnes pouted and narrowed his eyes. 'Four days I reckon,' he said.

'She'll die in four days?'

173

'You see she's swallowed about one hundred coproxomal tablets. They're powerful painkillers, a combination of paracetamol and distalgesic. The opiate component is what has flattened her while the rest has fairly comprehensively wrecked her liver. It will pack up soon and then they'll pack her up.'

'In four days?'

McInnes waggled his hand again. 'Give or take.'

'That's it? Nothing to be done?'

'We've put her on the national computerized transplant list but don't expect much.'

'Why not?'

'She's got a rare blood group. The chances of a donor being matched to her in the next few days are a good deal less than my chances of getting a decent night's sleep tonight.'

Fyfe decided he liked McInnes attitude. He would have liked to have bought him a drink and continued the irreverent conversation. 'You come straight to the point, don't you doc?'

'If you were a relative I would waffle and sympathize. But you're not, Chief Inspector. You're the filth so you get the dirty, unvarnished truth.'

'Thanks very much.'

'Any time. Just remember life's a female dog.'

'And then you die.'

'That's my best medical advice.' He nodded at the bed. 'In her case in about four days' time. In your case I would recommend a couple of pounds of the best steak on those eyes. Drape it over like a wet cloth.'

'I'll do that. Can I speak to her?'

'She's lapsing in and out of consciousness but you can try.' He beckoned to the nurse to come away from the bed. 'At least it won't hurt her.'

## 57

*Saturday, 01.10*

Outside the interview room Matthewson arranged for a doctor to be called to check on Wright. They had laid him out on the floor in the recovery position. He kept smiling. Moya, frustrated by Wright's obtuse replies to her questions, read the note that had been left with Fyfe's message on it. At least it offered something positive.

'We've found Norma,' she announced.

'Where?'

'In the royal infirmary. Some kind of overdose.'

'Alive?'

'Yes but she's probably unconscious too.'

'How did she get there?'

'Little brother Eddie found her at her flat apparently.'

'Did he now?'

They both had the same idea at the same time. They didn't have to articulate it into words to instantly understand what each was thinking. Little brother Eddie, playing the part of the poor innocent, unaware of everything that was going on around him. Maybe he wasn't so innocent after all. Maybe it was all an act to deflect suspicion. Maybe he was the puppet-master pulling the strings, and cutting them when it suited him.

'Everybody in that office was screwing somebody else,' Moya said. 'Now we know it was all to do with blackmail and insurance fraud. Is it possible Illingworth was simply the odd man out?'

'Anything's possible.'

'We don't want to jump to conclusions.' Moya restrained her enthusiasm, remembering how she had jumped in with both feet when Robert Ross presented himself as the prime suspect. 'Wright might be trying to pass the buck onto him or trying to drag him down as well?'

'It's possible.'

'Anything's possible you've just told me.'

The doctor arrived, blinking rapidly to fight off sleep. He was a middle-aged man with thin flyaway hair, a petulant mouth and the kind of resigned attitude that showed he had done this kind of thing a thousand times before. Matthewson knew him and introduced him by name to Moya. She didn't catch the name but didn't let on. They stood over him as he examined Wright on the floor, feeling for a pulse and then tut-tutting as he shone a thin torch beam into his eyeballs. Wright kept smiling.

'Any idea what knocked him out?' the doctor asked.

'Police brutality,' Matthewson said.

'Not enough bruises for that. I suppose we'd better get him down the road to hospital and waste some more taxpayer's money bringing him round.'

'Is he likely to wake up soon, doc?' Moya said.

'I doubt it. I've seen them sleep a week away when they're in a state like this. It depends on the tolerance they've built up. This guy I would say at first glance is a light to medium user. No injection marks so it's just for recreation. Cannabis definitely, probably a bit of cocaine. He's just gone over the score and pigged out. He'll survive.'

'Good,' Matthewson said. 'Then we can charge him.'

'The condemned man had a hearty blow-out,' the doctor said, snapping his bag shut and standing up. 'Can you get somebody to organize an amublance?'

'We'll do better than that,' Moya said. 'We'll run him along ourselves. We've got unfinished business at the hospital anyway.'

# 58

'Why did you do it, Norma?' Fyfe asked.

She watched him through cloudy, half-open eyes. Her skin was a deathly yellow, seemingly tissue-paper thin, tinged with pink around the eyelids and at the corners of her mouth. He didn't know if she could hear him, if she was even aware of him, but it looked as if she was struggling to say something. He leaned across the bed to get closer to her. He was so close to her mouth he could feel tiny exhalations of warm air on his cheek. He was looking down her body. The touches of air synchronized with the faint rising and falling of her chest. When she spoke her voice was weak but surprisingly clear through the wheeziness. It was like she was whispering inside his head.

'Why is an impossible question. It has a multitude of answers.'

'I'm Chief Inspector Fyfe, Norma. I'm a policeman. I need to know what happened.'

Fyfe raised his head. Her eyes were still half-closed. Only the shallow breathing indicated that she was alive. The signal of the heart monitor passed continually across the small screen. It reminded Fyfe of the dancing CD display lights in the cottage by the loch when they found Gilchrist's dangling body. Norma could not have had the strength to hang him up there. She had to have an accomplice. He leaned close to her again.

'Who made you do it Norma?'

'Nobody made me do it because it was always going to happen.'

'Who did it with you then? Who killed Laura?'

'He will die too. Very soon.'

'You still think you can see into the future, don't you Norma?'

'But I can.'

'Then why are you lying here like this?'

'I can see into the future. I can't change what I see.'

Fyfe felt the hairs on the nape of his neck bristle coldly. Norma's index finger was touching his forearm, hooking into it, pulling him closer. He couldn't lift his head. He could see her breathing getting faster and shallower. The monitor was speeding up.

'That's why I wrote those things in the magazine,' she whispered urgently. 'It was all true. All of it. All of it.'

'Only because you made it true, Norma. You put Laura on that rock after she was dead. You fulfilled your own prophecy, didn't you?'

'If you like.'

'And then you left the note because you wanted to be caught.'

'If you like.'

'You loved her, didn't you?'

'But I couldn't save her.'

The nurse touched his shoulder and motioned that he should leave. Fyfe pleaded for a few extra minutes, realizing that Norma was fading fast. The next time she lost consciousness she might never wake up again. He needed to find out as much as he could now. The nurse drew back reluctantly. Fyfe bent over Norma again.

'Who killed Laura? Was it Ron Gilchrist?'

'No. He was an irrelevance really.'

'Simon then? Simon Wright. Laura's ex-husband?'

'No. He didn't have the guts for it.'

'Then who? Not Eddie, your brother Eddie?'

'No. Not him.'

'There's nobody left. You're not going to tell me it was the bogey man, are you? That I won't believe.'

'There is somebody left. Think about it.'

Fyfe thought. He counted off the names. Process of elimination brought him to Douglas Lambert, Laura's father. He straightened up and shook his head, looking down on Norma. There was no indication that she was able to see him through her half-open eyes. Only when he leaned close once more and the rasping voice sounded inside his head was communication made.

'Laura always blamed him for the death of her little brother,' Norma whispered loudly. 'He was driving the car when it crashed. She humiliated him at every opportunity, reminded him as often as she could. It was an obsession with her. Her affair with me was only to annoy him. She didn't love me. She didn't love anyone.'

'Why did he allow her to stay in his house?'

'He was her father.'

'And he blamed himself anyway?'

'Something like that. I think he regarded Laura as some kind of divine retribution. Bit of a martyr, he was.'

'Why did he kill her?'

'She finally went too far. Told him she was pregnant and that Ron Gilchrist was the father. It was all lies but he wasn't to know. He had his suspicions and Ron was a prime suspect because he didn't exactly hide his infatuation. I backed Laura up. God knows, she had gone too far with me as well. I had my own plans for revenge but Doug got in first. I think I cheered when he flipped and hit her on the side of the head. I was bouncing on the bed while he strangled her. It was hugely exciting I remember.'

Fyfe could feel the tiny movements of Norma's lips, like something nibbling at his ear. Her voice was losing what little strength it had. She was slipping away fast.

'I tried to get Simon to help me but he froze. That had always been my plan, you see, me and Simon. He thought it was a blackmail plot. I let him think that. But it was too early for him. He wasn't ready. He didn't have the courage to go through with it. I went back to Doug. He had come to his senses, sort of. We worked out a rational plan. I would entice Ron to the cottage and we would kill him there. I knew about Doug and Pat Gilchrist, you see. With Ron out of the way that would leave him free to marry her, to be respectable again. That's all he wanted.'

'You must have known that scenario would never stand up.'

'I knew. Doug wanted to believe it was a way out for him. I convinced him he should believe it. It never was, of course.'

The nurse was pulling at Fyfe's arm. The heart monitor was pulsing fast. He resisted, staying close to Norma. Her index

179

finger fell away from his forearm. Her voice became even more distant.

'It had to be done. The prophecy. It had to be done.'

'And that's why you left the note?' Fyfe said.

'To give you a little help.'

'We needed it. Otherwise you might have got away with it.'

'I'll tell you something else, Chief Inspector. You will fulfil the rest of the prophecy.'

'How do I do that?'

'You will do it, Chief Inspector. You'll do it. Believe me.'

'I believe you,' Fyfe lied.

'Good.' Her voice dwindled to the tiniest of sounds. 'See you on the other side.'

## 59

*Saturday, 01.56*

Moya and Matthewson arrived at the Casualty Department as the human debris from a pub brawl was being swept up and put back together again. The waiting area was in uproar with friends and enemies staking out territory and forming protective circles round their injured. Insults were shouted across a narrow no-go space patrolled by the two uneasy security men. The threat of violence filled the atmosphere like electrical static. Police reinforcements had been called to stop things getting totally out of hand.

It had not been such a clever idea driving an unconscious Simon Wright to the hospital in their car. The doctor had rung up and then left them to it. Moya had sat in the back holding him up like some overgrown sleepy child. Now they couldn't get near the door because of a cluster of ambulances with blue lights flashing silently and causing a headache to build up in Moya's head. Matthewson went to find somebody who would listen to him, leaving Moya to look after Wright in the car. While she waited two police patrol cars, sirens braying, came hurtling down the slope from the main road and just managed to stop before colliding with the ambulances. The sirens were switched off but not the car-top warning panels, their patterns merging with intensified the silently screaming cacophony of flashing lights that were bouncing off every reflective surface and seemed to be visible even when Moya screwed her eyes tightly shut and clenched her teeth in impotent impatience.

It was more than fifteen minutes before Matthewson reappeared with a nurse and a porter pushing a wheelchair. Wright was quickly extracted from the car and taken inside to join the queue of bleeding, argumentative drunks.

Moya saw Eddie Illingworth through the crowd of people milling about in the waiting area. He was on his own, flat on his back and spread across three chairs. His mouth was wide open and he was snoring loudly. Moya walked determinedly through the crowd towards him. She restrained herself from kicking him but shook him roughly. The rhythm of his snoring was momentarily disturbed but she didn't succeed in waking him up. Instead he rolled off the chairs onto a carpet scarred by hundreds of cigarette burns and lay there face-down, snoring just as loudly and just as unaware of his surroundings. Moya felt herself pulled back by an arm and turned to be confronted by a small policewoman.

'No need for that,' the policewoman said. 'He's nothing to do with this. Leave him alone.'

'I know who he is, constable,' she shouted. 'I know exactly who he is.'

'And who are you?'

Moya paused to think more rationally for a second. Matthewson had completed the paperwork necessary to admit Wright and was making his way through the scattered bodies towards her. She searched in her bag for her identity card and showed it to the policewoman with an apologetic smile.

'You'll not get much out of Eddie for the time being, Inspector McBain,' she said. 'He's drunk as a skunk.'

'What about Norma? What kind of state is she in?'

'Much the same, according to the doctors. DCI Fyfe managed a few words with her before she went under. Only a few.'

'Where is he now?'

181

'He left before this rammy started.'

'Wise decision,' Matthewson said.

The hostile crowd was jostling and shoving. A fight broke out in one corner and a policeman's hat was knocked off. More uniforms arrived at the run. Truncheons were drawn. One man was wrestled to the floor and his nose slammed into it to quieten him as his hands were handcuffed behind his back. Beside him, Illingworth snored unconcernedly.

'Where did DCI Fyfe go?'

'He said he would meet you at the undertakers.'

'The undertakers? Lambert's place? Why? When?'

'He said to tell you when you arrived that he would be at the undertakers. That's all.'

'We'd better go then,' Moya said. 'There's nothing for us here. Watch Illingworth. Don't let him out of your sight.'

The policewoman looked down at Illingworth's prone body. 'That won't be too difficult,' she said.

## 60

*Saturday, 02.48*

Fyfe sat in his car opposite the blank windows of Lambert's the undertakers. The smeared colours of the constantly changing posters on the electronic hoarding above were reflected in the windscreen and the glossy wetness of the empty street. Jill sat in the passenger seat alongside him, staring straight ahead. Number Five lay on the rear seat, sound asleep. In the glove compartment was a sealed polystyrene tray containing a large slice of steak he had bought in an all-night shop on his way over.

He had seen a movement as he arrived, a twitch of the curtains at the first-floor window of Lambert's living-room. It had been no more than that, a flicker, hardly anything at all, but it was enough to convince Fyfe that Lambert was expecting him. Fyfe went over to what was probably Lambert's car, parked in the street. He examined the tyres one by one and found a shallow but distinctive s-shaped cut across the rear offside. He went back to his own car and waited. There was no hurry, he told himself. He reached over absent-mindedly and stroked the back of Jill's neck. No hurry at all.

Fyfe tried to think himself into Lambert's mind, tried to understand the feelings of guilt and shame that must have wracked him with the death of his young son. And how it must have been intensified a thousandfold every time his unforgiving daughter took delight in reminding him. A daughter who spurned his ambition for respectability, who wallowed in decadence and amorality and brought a lesbian lover to live under his own roof. And then, just for fun, she told him she was pregnant by an old family friend and laughed in his face.

Fyfe could imagine how the shame and the repressed anger must have been converted into a murderous blind fury that made him hit out, then seize her by the throat and squeeze until he had snuffed out her own life and the threatening seed of new life inside her. And then, insulated by a protective skin of unreality, how he had made one last desperate attempt to achieve the respectability he craved. He would exonerate himself by putting the blame on his friend Ron Gilchrist, who had made Laura pregnant anyway. And by doing so he would clear the way to marry the eminently respectable Pat, whose only excuse for refusing him was that she didn't want to hurt her husband.

It was all so simple and perfect. With Norma's encouragement, he put his plan into action. How was he to know that Norma had a warped death-wish and always intended that they should be found out? All she wanted to do was to act out the details of her own strange fantasy of Laura's death and then die herself as soon as she knew it was fully appreciated.

A sprinkling of raindrops landed on the windscreen, splitting the changing colours into a hundred separate pieces of chameleon light. Jill curled up in the seat and lay down, her tail under her chin. What would he do if it was him, Fyfe wondered? What would he do if things had unfolded differently and he had woken that morning in the flat to find Moya's cold dead body next to his?

He looked up at the window. Nothing moved but there was a light on behind the curtains. Lambert was in there alone. The skin of unreality would be flaking off. The inescapable realization of what he had done would be eating into him. He had no excuse and no justification. He was backed into a corner with nowhere to run. Retribution was parked outside. What would he do if he found himself in such a position, Fyfe wondered? He would want to be alone for a while. Fyfe could surely grant him that final request. There was no hurry. No hurry at all.

What would he have done, he kept thinking, if he had woken beside a dead Moya? Suppose her fancy man Dalglish had sneaked into the flat in the middle of the night and strangled her as Fyfe lay snoring. What would he have done? He would have panicked, tried to cover it up, packed her in the boot of the car and tried to find somewhere to hide the body. DI McBain? I dropped her off at the flat in the evening. Last I saw of her. And once begun, the lies would have continued until her body was discovered and the truth sprang up like a jack-in-the-box.

Weariness affected Fyfe. It had been a very long day. He rubbed his eyes carefully because of the tender bruising, then ran the palms of his hands more firmly over the rough stubble on his jaw. In front of him there were extra coloured lights among the raindrops on the windscreen. Beyond them the road and pavement seemed to slowly transform from flat to undulating. The shop fronts bulged outwards and the buildings leaned over until there was only a very narrow strip of sky above him.

Fyfe blinked and shook his head hard. The scene returned to normal, except that Moya's face was at the window beside him. She was tapping on the glass, mouthing something he could not hear. He pressed the switch and the window slid open. A moment's direct eye contact was enough to re-establish the professional boundaries. This was a murder inquiry. She was in charge. The evening's romantic diversion had not happened.

'Long time no see,' Fyfe said.

'Long enough for you to damage your other eye, I see. Why are we here?'

'Norma's the Bobby of recent legend. She's pointed the accusing finger.'

Moya turned and looked up at the first-floor window. 'What a bastard. His own daughter.'

'He had his reasons I suppose.'

'Is he in there?'

'I believe so. I was just waiting for reinforcements.'

Fyfe closed the window and got out of the car before Jill and Number Five had a chance to wake up properly. The dogs sat up and watched him and Moya and Matthewson cross the road and go to the side entrance that led up to the flat. Fyfe explained events as he understood them as they stood outside the door. It was locked and there was no answer to the bell.

'Are you sure he's there?' Moya demanded.

Fyfe nodded. 'I saw him at the window.'

They debated whether they should go through the rigmarole of contacting the duty manager before Matthewson put his shoulder to the door. Three hefty thumps and a straight-leg kick were enough to break the lock. Fyfe was first in, leading the way upstairs and into the living-room, Moya right behind him.

Lambert was lying on the floor. His legs were pulled up tight against his chest and there was an expression of such exquisite pain on his face that Fyfe's first thought was that he was lying there helpless with silent laughter. But he wasn't moving at all and the expression was fixed too, unchanging as though it was modelled out of wax. Moya shoved past him and knelt down beside Lambert, searching for a pulse in the neck.

'He's still alive,' she shouted. 'Call an ambulance.'

Matthewson went for the phone. Fyfe stood where he was, looking down on Moya. He was fascinated to see for the first time a tiny strawberry birthmark on the back of her left hand. He was thinking they should have waited outside just a little bit longer. If it had been him, that was how he would have wanted it to end.

# 61

The casualty waiting area at the hospital was empty and quiet. The chairs had been knocked out of their orderly arrangement and were strewn about haphazardly, like the aftermath on board a ship that has sailed through a bad storm. The light inside the tea and coffee machine flickered annoyingly. Moya and Fyfe sat side by side waiting for news of Lambert. Fyfe invented a story about walking into a door to explain the damage to his other eye. Moya didn't believe him. He told her about Norma's rare blood group and her guaranteed total liver failure in four days' time. She believed that.

Matthewson had vanished. A nurse carrying a clipboard passed by and asked them if they were Mr and Mrs Stewart. She looked puzzled when they denied it, wandering off talking to herself. A few minutes later baby-faced Dr McInnes appeared round the corner of the reception desk and they rose together as he began to walk towards them.

'What do you think then?' Fyfe asked Moya.

'I reckon he'll live.'

'I reckon he'll die. Remember the prophecy.'

'What?'

'It is right that my killer will die.'

Moya grunted. 'I think we have effectively demonstrated that there is no supernatural influence to the course of events under investigation.'

'Don't be so sure.'

'He's just a bad bastard like the rest of them.'

'He deserves to die then.'

'If only we all got what we deserved.'

'If only.'

They exchanged a look that took them both back to the New Town flat, and the bathroom when she had him backed up

186

against the sink. A smile almost broke the determined horizontal line of Moya's lips. Fyfe tried to raise his eyebrows in a humorous gesture but the bruised muscles round his eyes wouldn't respond. McInnes stood in front of them like a white-coated minister about to perform a marriage ceremony.

'Well, it was touch and go,' he said.

'And?' Moya prompted when McInnes showed no signs of continuing.

'He's gone.'

'You mean he's dead?'

'As a dodo.'

Fyfe nodded knowingly. He wouldn't say to Moya that he had told her but he thought it and rather enjoyed the guilty feeling of superiority it gave him. Moya darted an accusing glance at him. The brief paramedic panic at the funeral parlour and the wailing ambulance through the city streets had all been in vain. Fyfe could have told them at the time but nobody would have listened to him.

'What killed him?' Moya asked.

'A deadly cocktail of brandy, arsenic and nitrosulphuric acid.'

'Sounds exotic,' Fyfe said.

'Embalming fluid. Not the brandy but the other two. He was an undertaker I understand. Embalmed himself. Neat huh?'

'It was a close run thing. If he had been found maybe ten minutes earlier he might have stood a chance when we pumped him out. As it was he was dead in the ambulance.'

'Thanks doc.'

'I'm going to get some sleep now,' McInnes said. 'I'd be grateful if you didn't bring any more bodies in for a while. Remember my advice about those black eyes of yours.'

'Consider it done.'

McInnes shambled off. Fyfe stuck his hands in his pockets. Moya picked up her bag and looped it over her shoulder.

'That's that then,' she said.

'It is.'

'We didn't beat Isotonic's record for solving a murder but we got there in the end.'

'Just like the magazine said.'

'What do we do now?'

'You're in charge DI McBain but if it was me I would go home and get some sleep before we claim the credit and tackle the paperwork tomorrow.'

'Later today you mean.'

'Exactly.'

'Can you give me a lift?'

'I always stop for good-looking women.'

Fyfe drove Moya across the city. Jill sat on the floor between her legs all the way with her head in her lap. Number Five whined in the back because she was missing out.

'It's been good working with you,' Fyfe said, hoping it didn't sound too condescending.

'Likewise I'm sure.'

'We must do it again sometime.'

'Is that a prophecy?'

'Might be a threat.'

In the street outside the flat Moya kissed the dogs goodbye and climbed out of the car. It was almost dawn. The darkness was turning grey around them.

'What about me?' Fyfe said. 'Don't I get a farewell kiss?'

Moya hesitated half in and half out the car, facing him, her face framed in tumbling hair. This time she could not stop herself smiling.

'We had our chance, Dave,' she said. 'We missed it. Let's stay friends.'

'And colleagues.'

'That too.'

She kissed the tips of her fingers, held them up to her mouth and blew. Fyfe snatched at the air in front of his face and pressed the palm of his hand to his mouth. He watched Moya go round the car and mount the steps to the front door of his flat. He waited until it was opened and she had disappeared inside.

'Missed my chance there,' he told the dogs. 'Story of my life.'

# 62

Halfway home, halfway along an arrow-straight piece of road that descended into a shallow U-shaped valley, there was a layby screened from the road by grassy mounds. Dawn was breaking when Fyfe drove into it. The sky had turned a delicate shade of purple and a milk-white three quarter moon hung low on the foreshortened horizon.

'One last thing to do, girls,' he said to Jill and Number Five as he let them out to run. 'Then we can all go home and I can have a shave.'

He sat in his seat for several minutes, staring up at the moon, trying to make some kind of sense of the contours scrawled over the shadow-rich surface, seeing the thin line that described the perfect hidden circle. The air in the interior of the car was warm around him like the water of a deliciously warm bath. His head was sore. His injured eyes were throbbing. He phoned Sally and listened fondly to her sleep-slurred voice, anticipating her nearness.

'I'll be home soon, darling,' he said. 'Very soon.'

Her reply was unintelligible. Fyfe reached into the glove compartment and took out the piece of steak. He tore off the plastic wrapping and held the sweet-smelling meat in one hand as he got out of the car.

He walked over to where Jill and Number Five were sniffing in the grass. On the other side of the low mound that marked the edge of the lay-by a sheep fence had been trampled into the earth in a morass of hill-walkers' bootprints and rabbit droppings. The rotten posts had broken and lay on their sides with rusty wire stretching between them as if they were holding hands. Fyfe stepped over the fence onto a bare patch of earth.

Once more he looked up and the moon and its crescent seemed to shine even brighter. He tilted his head right back and draped the cold, heavy steak over his eyes. He began to howl, softly at first but then more loudly. Again and again the ululation came from his throat and soared towards the moon. The two dogs stopped sniffing at the grass and sat down where they were, silently looking across at him as if he was mad.